THE GOOD OLD ROCKING-HORSE

and other toyland tales

Illustrated by
Paul Crompton

World International Publishing Limited
Manchester

These stories were first published in Sunny Stories and Enid Blyton's Magazine between 1928 and 1959.

Published in Great Britain by World International Publishing Limited,
An Egmont Company, Egmont House, PO Box 111,
Great Ducie Street,
Manchester M60 3BL.
Printed in Italy.

British Library Cataloguing in Publication Data
Blyton, Enid 1897–1968
The good old rocking-horse and other toyland tales.
I. Title
823.912 [J]

ISBN 0–7498–0299–5

Cover illustration by Robin Lawrie

Contents

Enid Blyton

Enid Blyton was born in London in 1897. Her childhood was spent in Beckenham, Kent, and as a child she began to write poems, stories and plays. She trained to be a teacher but she devoted her whole life to being a children's author. Her first book was a collection of poems for children, published in 1922. In 1926 she began to write a weekly magazine for children called *Sunny Stories*, and it was here that many of her most popular stories and characters first appeared. The magazine was immensely popular and in 1953 it became *The Enid Blyton Magazine*.

She wrote more than 600 books for children and many of her most popular series are still published all over the world. Her books have been translated into over 30 languages. Enid Blyton died in 1968.

The good old rocking-horse

In the playroom there was a big old rocking-horse. His name was Dobbin, and he was on rockers that went to and fro, to and fro, when anyone rode on him.

He was a dear old horse, and it was very strange that the toys didn't like him! They were afraid of him – and it was all because of something that was quite an accident.

It happened like this.

One day the toy monkey fell off the shelf nearby, and went bump on to the floor. His long tail spread itself out and a bit of it went under one of the rocking-horse's rockers.

Well, that didn't matter a bit – until

John got up on to the horse and rocked to and fro. Then, of course, the rocking-horse pinched the monkey's tail hard every time he rocked over it, and the monkey sobbed and cried after John had gone to bed.

"You great, big, unkind thing!" sobbed the poor monkey, holding his tail between his paws. "You nearly squashed my tail in half. You hurt me dreadfully. I nearly squealed out loud when John was riding you. I don't like you one bit."

"Listen, Monkey," said the rocking-horse in his deep, gentle voice, "I didn't mean to do that. I didn't even know that your tail was there. And in any case I couldn't help it, because John rocked me so hard. But do believe me when I say that I am very, very sorry. I wouldn't have hurt you for the world!"

"I should just think you *are* sorry!" wept the monkey. "Oh, my poor tail! Whatever shall I do with it?"

The teddy bear came up with a

bandage. The baby doll came up with a bowl of water. They bathed the tail and then bound up the squashed end with the bandage. The monkey looked at his tail and felt rather grand when he saw how important it looked with a bandage round it.

It was quite better after a time – but somehow the toys really never forgave the rocking-horse, and he was very sad about it. He knew that he couldn't have helped rocking over the monkey's tail – it was really John's fault for leaving his monkey on the floor – but the toys never seemed to understand that.

So they didn't ask Dobbin to play games with them, and they never even said "yes" when he asked them to have a ride on his back. They just shook their heads and said "no". This hurt the rocking-horse very much, because there was nothing he liked better than giving people rides.

"They think I'm unkind, though I'm not," he thought sadly. "Well, I suppose they will always think the same and I must just put up with it."

Now the toys were very friendly with a little red squirrel who lived in the pine trees at the bottom of the garden. He often used to come leaping up to the windowsill to talk to them. Sometimes he even came right into the playroom and he was delighted one day when they got out one of the dolls' hair brushes and brushed his beautiful bushy tail for him.

"Oh, thank you," he said. "Thank you very much indeed. That's so kind of you. I'll bring you a present one day, Toys."

So when the autumn came he brought them a present. It was two pawsful of nuts! He had picked them from the hazel trees for the toys.

"Here you are," he said. "Nuts for you. They are most delicious! You must crack the hard shell and inside you will find a lovely white nut. I do hope you will like them. Goodbye!"

He sprang off to find some nuts for himself. He meant to hide some in cracks and corners, so that if he awoke in the cold winter days he might find his nuts and have a meal.

The toys looked at the nuts. They were so excited and pleased because they didn't often get any presents. They longed to eat the nuts and see what they tasted like.

The teddy put one into his mouth and tried to crack the shell. But he couldn't. It was much too hard. Then the brown toy dog tried to crack one. But even he couldn't! Then the toys threw the nuts hard on to the floor, but not one cracked.

"We shan't be able to eat the nuts," said the brown dog sadly. "They will be wasted!"

"Let us get the little hammer out of the toy tool-box," said the teddy bear. "Perhaps we can break the nuts with that."

So they looked for the toy hammer and they found it. They put a nut on the floor and hit it hard with the hammer. But the nut jumped away each time, unbroken. It was most tiresome.

Then the rocking-horse spoke up in his deep, gentle voice. "I can crack your nuts for you, Toys! If you will put them underneath my rockers I can rock over them and crack the shells! One of you must ride me to and fro, and then I can easily crack the nuts for you."

The toys all looked at one another. They badly wanted their nuts cracked, so they thought they would do as Dobbin said. They laid all the nuts in a row under his rockers. Then the teddy bear climbed up on the horse's back and began to rock him to and fro.

Crick-crack, crick-crack went all the nuts as the shells broke. Inside were the lovely white kernels, so sweet and delicious to eat!

"Thank you, Dobbin!" said the toys. The teddy bear patted him and slid down to get his nuts.

"That was a lovely ride I had!" he whispered to the other toys. "I wouldn't mind another!"

"Have as many as you like!" said Dobbin, who heard what the teddy said. "Are the nuts nice?"

"Delicious! Have one?" said the bear, and he held one up for Dobbin to nibble. "It was kind of you to crack them for us – very friendly indeed."

"I'm such a friendly person," said the rocking-horse sadly, "but you won't make friends with me. I would so much like to give you all a ride."

He looked so sad that the monkey suddenly felt very sorry for him. In a trice he had leapt up on to Dobbin's back.

"Gee-up!" he cried. "I'll be friends with you! Gee-up!"

And then, one after another, all the toys had a ride, and after that they were as friendly as could be. Wasn't it a good thing Dobbin offered to crack their nuts for them?

The toys go to the seaside

Once upon a time the goblin Peeko put his head in at the playroom window and cried, "Who wants a day at the seaside?"

The toys sat up with a jerk. They were all alone in the playroom, for Tom and Beryl, whose toys they were, had gone away to stay at their granny's. The toys were really feeling rather dull. A day at the seaside sounded simply gorgeous!

"How do we go?" asked the pink rabbit.

"By bus," said the goblin, grinning. "*My* bus. I bought it yesterday. Penny each all the way there."

"Oooh!" said the sailor doll, longingly. "I *would* like to see the sea. I've never been there – and it's dreadful to be a sailor doll and not to know what the sea is like, really it is!"

"Come on, then," said Peeko. "Climb out of the window, all of you. There's plenty of room in the bus."

So the pink rabbit, the sailor doll, the yellow duck, the walking-doll, the black dog and the blue teddy bear all climbed out of the window and got into the goblin's bus, which was standing on the path outside. The goblin took the wheel. The bus gave a roar and a jolt that sent the pink rabbit nearly through the roof – and it was off!

It was a fine journey to the sea. The goblin knew all the short cuts. It wasn't long before the sailor doll gave a yell and cried, "The sea! The sea!"

"Pooh!" said Peeko. "That's just a rain-puddle."

"Oh," said the sailor doll. But after a bit he shouted again. "The sea! The sea!"

"Pooh!" said the goblin. "That's just a duck-pond."

"But aren't those gulls sailing on it?" asked the doll.

"No, *ducks*!" said Peeko.

"Quack, quack!" said the yellow toy duck, and laughed loudly at the sailor doll. After that the doll didn't say anything at all, not even when they came to the real sea and saw it glittering and shining in the sun. He was afraid it might be a duck-pond too – or an extra big puddle!

They all tumbled out of the bus and ran on to the beach. "I'm off for a swim!" said the yellow duck.

"I'd like a sail in a boat!" said the sailor doll. "Oh! There's a nice little boat over there, just my size."

It belonged to a little boy. He had gone home to dinner and had forgotten to take his boat with him. The sailor doll ran to it, pushed it out to the sea, jumped aboard and was soon off for a fine sail. He *was* enjoying himself!

The pink rabbit thought he would like to make himself a burrow in the sand. It was always so difficult to dig a burrow in the playroom. Now he really would be able to make one! So he began to dig, and showered sand all over the blue teddy bear.

"Hi, hi, Pink Rabbit, what are you doing?" cried the bear. But the pink rabbit was already deep in a sandy tunnel, enjoying himself thoroughly, and didn't hear the bear's shout.

"I shall have a nap," said the blue teddy bear. "Don't disturb me, anybody."

He lay down on the soft yellow sand and shut his eyes. Soon a deep growly snore was heard. The black dog giggled and looked at the walking-doll. "Shall we bury him in sand?" he wuffed. "He would be so surprised when he woke up and found himself a sandy bear."

"Yes, let's," said the doll. So they began to bury the sleeping teddy in sand. They piled it over his legs, they piled it over his fat little tummy, they piled it over his arms. They didn't put any on his head, so all that could be seen of the bear was just his blunt blue nose sticking up. He did look funny.

"I'm off for a walk," said the walking-doll. "This beach is a good place to stretch my legs. I never can walk very far in the playroom – only round and round and round."

She set off over the beach, her long legs twinkling in and out.

The black dog was alone. What should he do?

"The sailor doll is sailing. The yellow duck is swimming. The pink rabbit is burrowing. The teddy bear is sleeping. The walking-doll is walking. I think I will go and sniff round for a big fat bone," said the black dog. So off he went.

Now when Peeko the goblin came on to the beach two or three hours later, to tell the toys that it was time to go home, do you think he could see a single one? No! There didn't seem to be anyone in sight at all! Peeko was annoyed.

"Just like them to disappear when it's time to go home," he said crossly. "Well, I suppose I must just wait for them, that's all. I'll sit down."

Peeko looked for a nice place to sit. He saw a soft-looking humpy bit of sand. It was really the teddy bear's tummy, buried in sand, but he didn't know that. He walked over to the humpy bit and sat right down in the middle of it.

The blue bear woke up with a jump.

"Oooourrrrrr," he growled, and sat up suddenly. The goblin fell over in a fright. The bear snapped at him and growled again. Then he saw it was Peeko.

"What do you mean by sitting down in the middle of me like that?" he said crossly.

"How should I know it was the middle of you when you were all buried in sand?" said Peeko.

"I wasn't," said the bear, in surprise, for he had no idea he had been buried.

"You were," said Peeko. "Just tell me this, Teddy – where in the world has everyone gone to? It's time to go home."

"Is it really?" said the bear, astonished. "Dear me, it seems as if we've only just come!"

"I don't see why you wanted to come at all if all you do is snore," said Peeko. "Waste of a penny, I call it!"

"Well, if you think that, I won't give you my penny," said the teddy, at once.

"Don't be silly," said the goblin. "Look here, Bear, if we don't start soon, it will be too late. What am I to do? I'd better go without you."

"Oh no, don't do that," said the bear in alarm. "I'll soon get the others back. We have a special whistle that we use when it's time to go home."

He pursed up his teddy-bear mouth and whistled. It was a shrill, loud whistle, and every one of the toys heard it. You should have seen them rushing back to the beach!

The sailor doll sailed his ship proudly to shore, jumped out, and pulled the ship on to the sand. He really did feel like a sailor now!

The yellow duck came quacking and swimming in, bobbing up and down in delight. She waddled up the beach, and shook her feathers, sending a shower of drops all over Peeko, who was most annoyed.

The walking-doll tore back across the beach. The black dog came running up, carrying an enormous bone in his mouth, very old and smelly. The toys looked at it in disgust.

"Where's the pink rabbit?" asked Peeko. "He *would* be last!"

The toys giggled. Peeko was standing just at the entrance of the pink rabbit's burrow, but he didn't know he was! The toys knew what would happen – and it did!

The pink rabbit had heard the bear's whistling. He was coming back along his burrow. He suddenly shot out, all legs and sand – and Peeko felt his legs bumped hard, and he sat down very suddenly! The pink rabbit had come out in a great hurry just between the goblin's legs. The toys laughed till they cried. Peeko was quite angry.

"First I sit on a hump that isn't a

hump and get a dreadful fright!" he said. "And then I get bowled over by a silly rabbit who comes out of the sand. Get into the bus all of you, before I say I won't take you home."

They all got into the bus. Most of them were tired and sleepy now, all except the teddy bear, who was very lively indeed – but then, he had been asleep all the time!

They climbed in at the playroom window. They each gave Peeko a penny, and he drove his bus away quietly and parked it under the lilac bush. The toys crept into the cupboard and sat as still as could be.

And when Tom and Beryl came back the next day from their granny's, they *were* surprised to see how well and brown their toys all looked.

"Just as if they had been to the seaside!" said Tom.

"Don't be silly, Tom!" said Beryl.

But he wasn't silly! They *had* been to the seaside!

The engine that ran away

Once there was a lovely wooden engine in the playroom. It was red with a blue funnel and blue wheels, and it had a dear little cab just big enough for a doll to stand inside.

At night the toys always ran to the wooden engine to ask him to give them rides round the playroom. Sometimes a doll would stand inside the cab and drive, sometimes the teddy bear and sometimes the pink rabbit.

But the wooden engine wasn't very friendly. "I don't want to give rides," he grumbled. "Get out of my cab, Teddy. I shall upset you if you try to drive me tonight. I'll run over the edge of the rug and jerk you out."

"Engines are made so that they can run along and pull things and give rides to people," said the teddy bear. "Don't be so bad tempered! It's good for you to run about at night. You'll get fat if you don't!"

"I shan't," said the engine and jerked the teddy bear so hard that he fell out. Then the toys were cross and they *all*

clambered on to the engine and made him carry every one of them.

"I shall run away," said the engine, sulkily. "I *won't* give you rides!" And will you believe it, the very next night he ran out of the playroom, down the passage, out of the garden door and into the garden!

"I'm free, I'm free!" he cried, bumping down the path. "I won't give rides any more. I'll go on a long, long journey by myself and have a lovely time!"

Now, the engine had six wooden wheels, but they were not meant to go over rough stones and tufts of grass. He went over such a big stone that quite suddenly the two back wheels came right off! The engine didn't notice it at first, and then he found that he was going rather clumsily. Oh dear – now he only had four wheels!

He went on down the path and squeezed through a hole in the fence at the bottom of the garden – but that was a silly thing to do because he broke off his funnel! He had to leave it behind, because he couldn't possibly put it on again!

On he went and on. "I feel funny without my funnel," he said to himself. "What shall I do if I ever want to send out smoke? I haven't got a funnel to blow through now!"

He bumped over a field, and suddenly ran into a big rabbit. "Hey there – what do you think *you're* doing?" cried the rabbit, angrily. "You bumped my tail."

"Get out of my way then," said the engine, rudely. That made the rabbit so angry that he chased the engine at top speed. It ran over a brick and oh dear – two more wheels broke off!

"Now I can hardly run at all," said the engine in alarm. "Oh dear, oh dear – four wheels gone, and my funnel, too. What bad luck!"

"To-whit-too-whoo!" said a big owl, flying overhead. "What's this crawling along? A new kind of rat? I'll attack it!"

And down swooped the owl and caught hold of the engine's little cab with its strong feet. The cab broke away in the owl's claws, and the poor engine hurried off without it, scared and trembling. The owl dropped the cab in disgust. "It wasn't a rat after all," it said.

The engine went on and on, and came to a very stony path indeed. Crack! Crack! Both its last wheels broke away, and the engine found itself sliding down a muddy bank, unable to stop itself. Splash! It went into a pond and floated there, looking very strange.

No wheels! No cab! Not even a funnel! Just a flat piece of wood and a round body – nothing else. No wonder the pixie who lived by the bank wondered what was falling down near her home.

"Save me, save me!" called the engine, floating away.

"Good gracious! What can it be?" said the pixie. She got a piece of string and made a loop at one end. She threw the loop over the body part of the engine and drew him back to shore. "Whatever are you?" she said.

"I'm an engine," said the poor, broken toy. "But I've lost my wheels and my cab and my funnel, so I feel very miserable indeed. I've run away, you see."

"Why did you run away?" said the pixie, drying the engine.

"Because I didn't like giving the toys a ride each night," said the engine.

"How mean of you!" said the pixie. "But I suppose you feel happier now that you have lost your six nice wheels and your cab and your lovely funnel. You can't give *anyone* a ride now."

"I *don't* feel happy," said the engine. "It's dreadful to have no wheels. And I hate not having a cab and a funnel. I wish I was back in the playroom, with all the things I've lost. I'd let the toys ride me all night long!"

"Would you really?" said the pixie. "Because if you *really* mean that I'll help you."

"I do mean it," said the engine. "I do, I do!"

Well, the pixie tied the bit of string to the body of the poor old engine and dragged it back the way he had come. First she found two wheels. Then she came to where the owl had dropped the cab. She picked that up, too. Then she found two more wheels, and soon she came to where the little blue funnel lay beside the fence. Up the garden she found the last two wheels.

"There!" she said, "I've found everything you lost. I've some magic with me and I'll put you right if you keep your promise."

"I will, truly I will," said the engine.

And then you should have seen the pixie using her magic! It was rather like blue Vaseline, and she rubbed it on the wheels and the funnel and the cab and stuck them back in their proper places.

Soon the engine felt quite himself again!

"Oh, thank you," he said, gratefully. "I feel like an engine again now. It's lovely. Can I give you a ride?"

"Oh yes!" said the pixie, and she stepped into the little cab. She could drive beautifully! She drove the engine in at the garden door, up the passage and back to the playroom. Well, well – how clever of her!

"Toys! I've brought the runaway engine back to you!" she said. "He's nice and kind now – but if he ever says he won't give you rides, look out! Because then the magic that keeps his wheels and his cab and his funnel on will vanish away – and they will all fall off on to the floor!"

And now the toys take it in turns to drive the wooden engine round and round the playroom every night – and so far he has still got all his wheels and his cab and his funnel. I do hope he doesn't lose them, don't you?

The clown's little trick

In John's playroom were all kinds of toys, from the big rocking-horse down to the tiny clockwork mouse. They lived together happily and were kind and good to one another, just as John was kind to them.

But one day the fat little toy elephant wasn't so good after all. John had some little chocolate sweets and he seemed to enjoy eating them very much. The toy elephant watched him and wished he could taste one.

"Don't eat any more, John," said his mother. "You must make them last all the week – three a day, I should think."

John put them away on the bottom shelf of his little bookcase. The toy elephant saw exactly where he put them. And that night, in the dark, he left the toy cupboard, walked across the strip of lino, over the carpet, to the little bookcase. He felt about with his trunk and found the paper bag.

He put his trunk inside and felt the

little chocolates there. He got hold of one with his trunk and popped it into his mouth.

"My – it's good!" he whispered to himself. "Very, very good. I like it. Tomorrow night I'll fetch another."

He went back to the toy cupboard, stood himself in a corner and finished eating the sweet. All night long he tasted the flavour of it, and was happy. He didn't think how naughty he had been to take it.

The next night he did the same, putting his little trunk into the bag and pulling out a sweet. He ate it, and then he took another. Nobody saw him. He just stood there in the dark and enjoyed himself.

But John soon found that someone was taking his sweets. He looked sternly at his toys.

"Toys," he said, "it's very sad, but *one* of you is taking my sweets at night. Don't do it. It's very, very wrong."

The toys were dreadfully upset. They

looked at one another when John had gone out for a walk.

"Can one of us be so horrid?" they said. "Who is it? Let him own up at once!"

But the fat little elephant said nothing. He didn't even go red. He wasn't a bit ashamed of himself. And that night he crept off to the paper bag and took two more sweets! He really did.

John was very sad the next day. He looked at the teddy bear, the clockwork clown, the mouse, the monkey, the elephant, the pink cat, the black dog and all the rest of them.

"If it happens again I am afraid I shall have to lock the toy cupboard door, so that none of you can get out at night," he said.

This was a horrid threat. The toys did so love to get out of the cupboard and play around sometimes when John was in bed. When the moon shone in at the window they often had a dance. It would be dreadful if John really did lock the cupboard.

When John had gone out of the room the clockwork clown stood up. "We simply *must* find out who is the thief," he said. "I am not going to let us *all* be punished for something that only *one* of us does! Let that one own up now before it is too late. For I warn him, I shall find him out."

The toy elephant didn't say a word. The clown frowned. "Very well," he said. "It will be very, very bad for the thief when I find him out."

Now, that night the clown did a funny thing. He crept into the larder and found the pot of honey there. He dipped in a paint-brush and hurried down to the floor again. He carefully painted the bit of shiny lino outside the toy cupboard with the honey on the brush. It made it very sticky indeed.

Then the clown went to the breadboard in the playroom cupboard and collected all the crumbs he found there. He took them to the little bookcase and scattered them just in front of the place where the paper sweet bag was kept.

Then he hurried back to the toy cupboard and sat down beside the teddy bear. He didn't tell anyone at all what he had done.

The toys were tired that night. John had played with them a lot that day. They fell asleep and slept soundly, all but the fat little elephant, who was waiting to go and get another sweet. When he was sure everyone was asleep, he crept out of the cupboard as usual. His four feet stepped on the honey. Then, with sticky feet, he padded over to the bookcase and put out his trunk to the sweet bag.

He trod on the scattered crumbs. They stuck to his feet, but he didn't know it. He took a sweet and padded back to the toy cupboard. He spent a long time enjoying the little chocolate.

Now, just at dawn, when a silvery light was coming in through the window, the clockwork clown woke all the toys up.

"Wake up," he said, and his voice sounded so stern that the toys were alarmed.

"What's the matter?" they said.

"I am going to show you who the thief is," said the clown. "I myself don't know who it is yet, but I soon *shall* know! Everyone sit down, please, and show me the soles of your feet!"

In great surprise all the toys did as they were told, and the clown looked at their feet quickly. And, of course, when he came to the elephant's feet, he saw the little crumbs sticking there, and smelt the honey on them, too!

"Here is the thief!" he cried. "Bad little elephant! Look, toys, he has crumbs stuck to his feet! You see, I spread honey just outside the cupboard, and scattered crumbs in front of the bookcase! And the elephant walked over the honey and the crumbs stuck to his feet! So now we know who the thief is! Bad little elephant!"

The toys were angry with the elephant. They turned him out of the toy cupboard. They made him go and stand in front of the sweet bag, so that John would know who the thief was, when he came in.

And he did, of course. "So *you* were the bad little thief!" he said. "I'm ashamed of you. I won't play with you any more!"

And the fat little elephant cried tears into the brick-box at the back of the toy cupboard, and made quite a puddle there.

"Serves you right," said the clown. "We shan't play with you either for a night or two. Perhaps you will think twice the next time you want to take things that don't belong to you!"

It was a clever trick of the clown's, wasn't it?

The clockwork kangaroo

The toys in Jackie's playroom were very happy together till the clockwork kangaroo came. Jackie had a big brown bear on wheels, a horse and a cart, a sailor doll, and a few other toys who lived together in the toy cupboard.

At night the sailor doll took the horse out of the cart, so that he could run free. In return the horse gave the doll a ride round the playroom. He loved to gallop about, and his hooves made a tiny pattering noise on the floor. Once when Jackie woke up, he heard the noise, but he thought it was the rain pattering outside! If he had looked into the playroom he would have seen that it was the horse.

The bear got the sailor doll to oil his wheels so that he could run quietly about at night without making any noise. The train didn't make much noise because it didn't run on its rails at night, but just anywhere it liked on the carpet.

And then the jumping kangaroo came. It was a very clever toy really, because its clockwork made it jump high in the air just as a real kangaroo does. How it could jump!

"Hallo!" said the kangaroo, the first night. "How are you all? I'm a jumping kangaroo."

"Oh, really, how interesting!" said the bear politely. "How far can you jump?"

"I'll show you," said the kangaroo. He sprang high into the air – and landed, bang, on the bear's nose!

"Please don't do that again," said the bear crossly, shaking the kangaroo off his nose.

The kangaroo sprang high into the air once more – and this time he landed on the engine of the train with such a crash that he bent the little funnel.

"Look what you've done!" said the train angrily. "I was very proud of my funnel. Now you've spoilt it. I don't look like a real train any more!"

The kangaroo leapt about till his clockwork was run down. Then, because no one would wind him up, he sat in a corner and sulked. He just couldn't reach his own key with his paws, which was a very good thing.

He made friends with Sam, a tiny doll whom nobody liked much, and Sam was always ready to wind him up. After that the toys didn't have a very good time at night, for the kangaroo was always jumping out at them from somewhere.

"He really is a *nuisance*," said the bear, rattling his four wheels crossly.

"So is Sam," said the sailor doll. "Always winding up the kangaroo so that he can jump on us."

"I wish the kangaroo had never come to our playroom," said the train. "We were as happy as could be before."

"Can't we get rid of him?" asked the horse. "Last night he jumped on my back and frightened me so much that I galloped three times round the playroom with him without stopping – and then he grinned and said, 'Thanks for the ride!' Horrid creature!"

"I wish he'd jump into the waste-paper basket!" said the bear. "That's deep – and he couldn't get out of there."

"Then he would be emptied into the dustbin the next morning and that would be the end of him," said the sailor doll. "That's an idea!"

"What do you mean?" asked the bear.

"I'll think of some plan with the waste-paper basket," said the doll. "Don't speak to me for a minute."

So he thought hard – and then he grinned round at the others. He looked round to make sure that the kangaroo was not near, and then he whispered to the others.

"Listen!" he said. "Tomorrow night we'll pretend to have a jumping-match to see who can jump the farthest. And when it comes to the kangaroo's turn to jump, we'll quickly swing out the basket – and he'll jump right into it."

"Oh, good!" said the bear. "Let's do it."

So the next night the toys all began talking about a jumping-match, and, of course, the kangaroo came along in great excitement, for he felt sure that he would be able to win the match easily.

"This is the jumping-off place," said the sailor doll, drawing a little line on the carpet with a piece of white chalk. "And we'll draw a white line to show where everyone jumps to – and the one who jumps the farthest shall win the prize."

"What is the prize?" asked the kangaroo at once.

"The prize is a chocolate," said the bear. The kangaroo was pleased. He wanted to have his turn first.

"No," said the bear. "Smallest ones first. Come on, Sam."

Sam stood on the chalk-line, grinning. He jumped – quite a good jump for such a tiny doll. The bear drew a chalk-line at the spot where he landed. "Now you, Ball!" he called. The red ball rolled up. It bounced off the chalk-line and did a very good jump indeed. The bear drew another line.

"That's fine, Ball," he said. "I believe you will win."

"No, he won't!" cried the kangaroo at once. "Let *me* try now!"

"It's not your turn," said the bear. "Train, come on."

The engine ran up and stood with its front wheels on the chalk-line. It gave a puff and jumped – but it fell right over on to its side with a clatter.

"Goodness! What a noise!" said the bear. "That wasn't a very good jump, Engine. Have you hurt yourself?"

"No," said the engine, and ran off into a corner on its six wheels to watch what was going to happen. The sailor doll jumped next – and his was a splendid jump, even better than the ball's. The kangaroo was so impatient to show that his jump would be even finer that he pushed everyone else out of the way and stood on the chalk-line himself, quite determined to win the prize.

"Now's the time to catch him!" whispered the bear to the sailor doll. "Where's the waste-paper basket?"

"I've got it ready under the table," whispered back the doll. "I'll go and push it out just as the kangaroo jumps! Don't say 'one, two, three, jump' till I'm ready."

The sailor doll ran under the table to the tall waste-paper basket. He took hold of it, ready to push it out. The bear saw that he was ready and counted for the kangaroo. "Are you ready? Now, one, two, three, JUMP!"

The kangaroo jumped. My, he did jump well! The doll saw him sailing through the air as if he had wings –

and then with a hard push the waste-paper basket was set right under the kangaroo – and he fell into it, plomp!

He was *most* surprised. He sat down on some apple-peel and torn-up paper and blinked his eyes in astonishment. "What's this?" he thought. "What's this?"

"Got him!" said the sailor doll in delight. All the toys danced round the basket in joy, except Sam, and he was cross. But he couldn't do anything at all.

"I say! I've fallen into the waste-paper basket," called the kangaroo, trying to scramble out. "This is most extraordinary."

"Yes, isn't it," giggled the sailor doll. "Didn't you see it there?"

"No, I didn't," said the kangaroo, puzzled. "It just seemed to come underneath me. I say, help me out, somebody."

But nobody did. Sam was too small to help, and the others wouldn't even try.

The kangaroo tried to jump out. He leapt higher and higher – but the basket was tall and he just couldn't jump over the top. He began to get frightened.

"My clockwork is nearly run down," he cried. "I can't jump out. Help me, do help me. I hate being mixed up with apple-peel, and paper, and dead flowers."

"Serves you right," said the bear gruffly. "You are a nuisance – and the right place for nuisances is the waste-paper basket or the dustbin."

The kangaroo began to cry. His clockwork had now run down and he could jump no more. He smelt of apple-peel. He was very unhappy because he knew that the basket was emptied into the dustbin every morning.

He began to scramble round and round the basket, like a goldfish swimming round a bowl. The toys giggled. The kangaroo had often frightened *them* – and now he was frightened himself. He would know what a horrid feeling it was.

Sam felt sorry for his friend, but he couldn't do anything to help him. "Oh, Kangy, I think the other toys have done this on purpose," he said sadly. "They have punished you for being naughty to them."

Well, the night went on, and the morning came – and Jane came to clean the playroom. She carried away the basket to empty it into the dustbin. And then the toys began to feel rather dreadful.

"I don't much like to think of Kangaroo in the smelly old dustbin," said the sailor doll. "What happens to things in the dustbin?"

"I don't know," said the bear. "Do you think he is very unhappy?"

Certainly the kangaroo was *most* unhappy. Jane had emptied him into the dustbin, and he had fallen on to a pile of wet tea-leaves, which stuck all over him.

"If only I had just one more jump left!" sighed the kangaroo sadly. "The next time anyone takes the lid off the dustbin I could jump out, for I am near the top."

Just as he spoke, Jane came to put some cinders there. She took off the lid and emptied the pan of cinders all over the kangaroo. He gathered himself together and did one last jump. Out he leapt – and Jane gave a yell.

"My gracious! What's this leaping about?"

She bent down and picked up the kangaroo. "Well, if it isn't the clockwork kangaroo. He must have got in here by mistake. I'll take him back to the playroom."

She took him back. Jackie wasn't there, so she put the dirty, cindery toy on the floor and left him there. He groaned, and the toys peeped out at him. At first they didn't know who it was, for the kangaroo was so dirty and so spotted with tea-leaves.

"Toys!" groaned the kangaroo. "Help me. I'm sorry I ever annoyed you. Do, do help me."

The toys were so pleased to think that the kangaroo was back that they all rushed to help him. They washed him. They brushed him. In fact, they couldn't do enough for him, and he almost cried for joy.

"It was dreadful in the dustbin," he said. "Really dreadful. Don't send me there any more. I'll never behave so badly again."

"Well, perhaps we've behaved badly too," said the sailor doll, ashamed. "You be kind to us, Kangaroo, and we'll be kind to you. There's nothing like kindness, you know."

Now the kangaroo never leaps on anyone, but instead he gives the sailor doll and Sam piggy-backs when he jumps – which is really *most* exciting for them. Didn't he have a horrid adventure?

The green plush duck

The green plush duck lived in the playroom with all the other toys. She had green plush wings, a green plush back, a red plush throat, a yellow beak and yellow legs; and a most beautiful voice that said "Quack!" very loudly when you pressed her in the middle.

Now none of the other toys had much voice. The teddy bear had only a very small growl because he had been so often pressed in the middle that his growl had nearly worn out. Emmeline, the baby doll, once had a voice that said "Mamma!" but when someone trod on her by accident one day her voice went wrong. And the rabbit never had a

growl or a squeak at all, though he pretended he had.

But, of course, when the playroom was in darkness and only the dying fire lighted up the room all the toys had lots to say! Their squeaks, growls and "Mammas" were only for the daytime – when day was gone they used their own proper little voices, and what a chatter there was!

Now it happened one evening that the green plush duck was feeling rather grand. Paul, the little boy the toys all belonged to, had had a friend to tea, and Margaret, the little friend, liked the plush duck best of all his toys. She had let the duck sit by her at teatime, and had made her quack quite a hundred times, if not more!

So no wonder the plush duck was feeling grand. Margaret had said that her quack was just like a real duck's and that she was the nicest duck in the world. So the plush duck was quite ready to be queen of the playroom that evening!

"Did you hear what Margaret said about me?" she said to the other toys. "She said my quack was . . ."

"Yes, we heard it," said the teddy bear, rather crossly. "We don't want to hear it again. Forget it, Duck."

"Forget it!" said the duck, in surprise. "Why should I forget it? I don't want to forget it, I want to remember it all my life. Why, Margaret said I was . . ."

"Oh do stop boasting!" said the rabbit. "And don't start quacking, for goodness sake. We've had enough of that awful noise today!"

"Well, I never! Awful noise indeed!" said the plush duck angrily. "Why, let me tell you this, Margaret said that I was the nicest duck in the world!"

"Well, you're not," said Emmeline, the doll. "Margaret can't have seen many ducks, or she wouldn't have said a silly thing like that. You're not a bit like a duck, not a bit! I have seen plenty of real live ducks, and they were all white.

You are a dreadful green colour, and you have a terrible quack that we're all tired of hearing, so now please be quiet."

Well, the plush duck was so angry to hear all that that she hardly knew what to say. Then she quacked very loudly indeed and said:

"So I'm not like a real duck, you say! Well, I am, so there! I can do everything a real duck can do, and I wish I *was* a real duck, so that I could live on the pond and not with nasty horrid toys like *you*!"

"Can you lay eggs?" asked the teddy bear.

"Of course not," said the plush duck.

"Well, a real duck can, so you're not like a real duck!" said the teddy.

"Can you swim?" asked the rabbit.

The plush duck didn't know. She had never tried.

"I expect so," she said at last. "I'm *sure* I could if I tried."

"Can you eat frogs?" asked Emmeline.

"Ooh, how horrid! I'm sure I don't want to!" said the plush duck, feeling quite ill.

"You can't lay eggs, you can't swim, you can't eat frogs, so you're not a *bit* like a real duck!" said the teddy. "Ha ha!"

"Ha ha!" said all the others.

The plush duck turned red with rage.

"I tell you I *am* like a real duck, only much nicer," she said. "I expect I *could* lay eggs and do everything else if I tried – but I've never tried."

"Well, try to lay an egg now," said Emmeline. So the plush duck solemnly sat down and tried hard to lay an egg. But it wasn't a bit of good, she couldn't. She was very disappointed.

"Well, eat a frog," said the rabbit.

"Get me one, and I will," said the plush duck. But nobody knew where to get a frog, or how to make it go to the playroom if they found one, so they told the plush duck they would take her word for that.

"Show us how you can swim," said the teddy.

"But where can I swim?" asked the duck. "There isn't a pond anywhere near, and the bathroom is too far away for us all to go there."

"You can swim in the tank belonging to the goldfish, up on that shelf there!" cried Emmeline, pointing to where the four goldfish swam slowly about in the big glass tank of water. But the plush duck didn't like the idea of that at all!

"Oh, I don't think I'll try tonight," she said. "The goldfish might not like it."

"You're afraid!" cried everyone. "You've told a story! You can't swim! You're not a *bit* like a real duck!"

This made the plush duck so angry that she at once climbed up to the shelf where the glass tank was, and popped into the water. For a moment or two she floated upright, and she was delighted.

"I *can* swim!" she called. But oh dear me, whatever was happening? Why, the water soaked into her plush skin and got right into the filling she was stuffed with. And she turned over and began to sink. How frightened she was – and how frightened the toys were too!

"Help, help!" cried the poor plush duck. "I'm sinking, I'm sinking! Help!"

The goldfish nibbled at her with their red mouths. The toys watched in horror. Whatever could they do? Then who do you think came forward to help? The three little plastic frogs that Paul floated in his bath each night! They had sat as quiet as could be all through the quarrel, because they were only small toys, and didn't like to speak. Also they had felt rather afraid in case the plush duck had offered to eat them instead of real frogs.

But they were brave, and they made up their minds to help. They jumped up to the shelf, and leapt into the tank of water. They dived underneath the poor frightened duck, and soon brought her to the surface again. The teddy and the rabbit pulled her out, and, dripping wet, she jumped down to the floor again.

"We're ever so sorry we teased you," said the bear, frightened. "Do forgive us."

"I'm not like a real duck," said the plush duck, sorrowfully. "I can't even swim."

"No, but you can quack," said the rabbit, anxious to make everything right again. "Quack, Duck, and let us hear your wonderful voice."

But what a dreadful thing! The water had got into the plush duck's quack, and she couldn't say a word. Not a single quack could she quack! She *was* upset. The water was very cold and she was shivering. The toys were afraid she would catch a dreadful cold, so they took her near the fire. The teddy was very brave and poked the fire well to make it flame up.

The duck gradually got dry, but she was still sad.

"I've not even got my quack now," she said with tears in her big glass eyes. "I can't swim, I can't lay eggs, I can't eat frogs, I can't even quack. I might as well be in the dustbin!"

"You mustn't say that!" said the toys, shocked. "Cheer up! We'll make you queen of the nursery, even if you *can't* quack!"

So they made the plush duck queen, but that didn't make her feel very happy, because she was so miserable about her lost quack.

But hip hurrah! In the morning when Paul came into the playroom to play, and pressed her in the middle, her quack had come back! "Quack!" she said, even more loudly than before! The water had dried out, and her quack was better than ever.

So now she is very happy. She is still queen of the playroom and her quack is just the same – but there's just one thing she won't do; she won't go anywhere near the tank of goldfish, and I'm not surprised, are you?

The cuckoo in the clock

In the playroom on the wall hung a cuckoo clock. Every hour the little wooden cuckoo sprang out of the little door at the top and called "Cuckoo!" very loudly indeed. Then it went back into its tiny room inside the clock and stayed there all by itself until the next hour came.

The wooden cuckoo was very lonely. There was nothing to do inside the clock except look at all the wheels going round, and he was tired of that. He was a most intelligent little cuckoo, and when the children talked near the clock, he listened to every word, and learnt quite a lot.

He knew when the bluebells were out

in the wood, for he had heard Lulu say that she was going bluebelling. And he knew that seven times six are forty-two, because once Barbara had to say it twelve times running because she hadn't learnt it properly the day before.

So you see he was quite a wise little cuckoo, considering that he lived in a tiny room inside a clock all day long. He knew many things, and he longed to talk to someone in the big world outside.

But nobody ever came to see him. The children had heard him cuckoo so often that they didn't think anything about him, and except when the clock was dusted each morning nobody came near him at all.

And then one night a wonderful thing happened. The little fairy Pitapat asked all the toys in the toy cupboard to a party at midnight! What excitement there was!

The teddy bear, the sailor doll and the baby doll all got themselves as clean and smart as could be. The wooden

Dutch doll scrubbed her rosy face clean, and the Japanese doll tied her sash in a pretty bow. The soldiers marched out of their box, and just as midnight came, the fairy Pitapat flew in at the window!

The cuckoo had to pop out at that moment to cuckoo twelve times, so he had a fine view of everything. He thought that Pitapat looked the dearest little fairy in the world – and then, dear me, his heart nearly stood still!

For Pitapat looked up at the clock, and saw him! She laughed and said: "Oh, what a lovely little cuckoo! And what a beautiful voice he has! I must ask him to come to my party."

She flew up to the clock, and asked the cuckoo to come to the party. He trembled with delight, and said yes, he would love to come. So down he flew among the toys and soon he was quite at home with them.

The party was in full swing and everyone was having a lovely time, when suddenly the door was slowly pushed open. Pitapat saw it first and she gave a little scream of fright.

"Quick!" she said. "Someone's coming! Back to your cupboard, all you toys!"

The toys scuttled back to the cupboard as fast as could be, just as Whiskers, the big black cat, put his head round the door. He saw something moving and made a pounce! And oh my, he caught poor little Pitapat, who was just going to fly away out of the window.

The cuckoo had flown safely up to his little room in the clock, and he peeped out when he heard Pitapat cry out. When he saw that Whiskers had got her, he didn't know *what* to do! He was terrified of cats – but he simply couldn't bear to think that Pitapat was in danger, with no one to help her at all.

So with a very loud "Cuckoo" indeed he flew bravely down to the floor. With his wooden beak he caught hold of Whiskers' tail and pulled and pulled and pulled. Whiskers couldn't think what it was that was tugging so hard at his tail, and he looked round to see.

In a trice the cuckoo flew to Pitapat, and picked her up in his claws. He flew to his clock, and, very much out of breath, put the little fairy down just inside his tiny room. Whiskers gave a mew of disgust when he found that the fairy had gone, and jumped out of the window.

The moon sent a ray of light to the cuckoo, and he could see Pitapat quite plainly. She looked very ill, and was as white as a snowdrop. The cuckoo felt certain that she ought to be in bed. But there was no bed in his little room!

Then he suddenly thought of the tiny bed in the small dolls' house in the toy cupboard. He flew down and asked the sailor doll to get it out for him. It was not long before he had the little bed in his beak, and was flying with it back to the clock.

He popped Pitapat into bed, and then fetched her a cup of milk from the dolls' house larder. She said she felt much better, and thanked him. Then she put her golden head down on the pillow and fell fast asleep. How pleased the cuckoo was that he had rescued her! He thought that she really was the loveliest little creature that he had ever seen.

For a whole week she stayed with him, and they talked and laughed together merrily. The cuckoo felt very sad when the week drew near to an end, for he really didn't know *what* he would do without his tiny friend. He knew that he would be lonelier than ever.

Then a wonderful idea came to him. If only Pitapat would marry him, they could live together always and he wouldn't be lonely any more! But would a fairy like to live in a tiny room inside a clock with a funny old wooden cuckoo? The cuckoo shook his head, and felt certain that she wouldn't. And a big tear came into one of his eyes and rolled down his beak.

Pitapat saw it, and ran to him. She put her arms round his neck and begged him to tell her why he was sad.

"I am sad and unhappy because soon you will go away, and I shall be all alone again," said the cuckoo. "I love you very much, Pitapat, and I wish I wasn't an ugly old wooden cuckoo with a stupid cuckooing voice, living in a tiny room inside a clock. Perhaps if I were a beautiful robin or a singing thrush you would marry me and we would live happily ever after."

"You aren't ugly and old!" cried the fairy, "and your voice is the loveliest I have ever heard! You are nicer than any robin or thrush, for you are the kindest bird I have ever met! And I will marry you tomorrow, and live with you in your clock!"

Well, the cuckoo could hardly believe in his good fortune! They asked all the toys to a wedding party, and Pitapat bought the cuckoo a blue bow to wear round his neck so that he looked very grand indeed. And after the party they went back to the clock and danced a happy jig together round the little room.

"I can make this room lovely!" said the fairy happily. "I will have blue curtains at the windows, and a tiny pot of geraniums underneath. I will get some little red chairs and a tiny table to match. Oh, we will have a lovely little house here, Cuckoo!"

She set to work, and she made the dearest little place you ever saw. The cuckoo loved it, and one day when Pitapat had brought a new blue carpet and put it down, he was so pleased that he quite forgot to spring out of his door at ten o'clock and cuckoo!

There was no one in the playroom but Barbara, and she was most surprised to find that the cuckoo didn't come out and cuckoo. She got a chair and put it under the clock. Then she stood on it and opened the little door.

And, to her very great surprise and delight, she saw Pitapat's little room, so bright and pretty, and the cuckoo and Pitapat sitting down to a cup of cocoa and a biscuit each! Weren't they surprised to see their door open and Barbara's two big eyes looking in!

"Don't tell our secret, Barbara dear!" cried Pitapat. "We are so happy. *Don't* tell our secret! Please! Please!"

"I'll keep your secret," promised Barbara. "But please do let me peep into your dear little house each day. It is so little and lovely."

"You can do that and welcome," said the cuckoo, and he got up and bowed.

So every day when there is no one in the playroom Barbara peeps into the cuckoo's home in the clock; and you will be glad to know that she has kept her word – she hasn't told a single soul the secret!

The elf in the playroom

Just outside the playroom window there was a climbing rose. It was very old, and had a thick twisted trunk, and hundreds and hundreds of leaves. In the summer it blossomed out, and was red with sweet-smelling roses.

In one of the thickest parts of the climbing rose lived a small elf called Lissome. She was a dear little thing with two long wings rather like a dragonfly's, which made a whirring noise when she flew.

Lissome was lonely, for no other elves lived in the garden. They were afraid of the two children who lived in the house. They were twin girls called Lucy and Jane, and they were rough and rude.

So no elves lived near them, except Lissome, who felt quite safe from them, high up in the climbing rose.

All the same it was a lonely life there. The sparrows sometimes came and talked to her. The robin had a song for her, and sometimes the summer butterflies and bees fluttered round and told her the news.

When she discovered that there were toys in the playroom who came alive at night and played merrily with each other, she was simply delighted!

She peeped in one night at the window and they all saw her!

"Look! An elf!" said the brown bear. "Let's ask her in!"

So in she flew on her long wings and smiled at all the wondering toys. There were the brown bear, the blue rabbit, three dolls, the black dog, the brown dog, and the pink cat. So there were a good many toys to play with!

Every night Lissome went to play in the playroom. All the toys loved her, for she was merry and kind. They played hide-and-seek, and catch, and hunt the slipper, and hunt the thimble, and a great many other games, too – the kind you play when you go to a party.

"You are lucky to be able to fly out of the window at dawn," said the brown bear one night. "We wish we could too!"

"Why?" said Lissome in surprise.

"Well, Lucy and Jane are such rough children," said the brown bear. "Look at my arm! It's almost off! The two children both wanted to play with me today, so they pulled and pulled – and my arm nearly came off! Whatever shall I do when it does?"

"I *am* sorry," said Lissome.

"And look at my tail," said the pink cat. "Lucy twisted it and twisted it today – and that's nearly off too. It may drop off at any minute! And who wants a cat without a tail?"

"You know, Toys, if you could lend me a needle and cotton, thimble and scissors, I think I could mend you," said Lissome. "I'm quite good at sewing."

"Are you really?" said the brown bear joyfully. "Well, here is the work-basket. It's got a lot of sewing things in it. Take what you want."

So Lissome took out a thimble which, however, was far too big, so she couldn't wear it. She took a tiny needle and threaded it, and she found a pair of scissors. Then she set to work.

She sewed the bear's arm beautifully. He was very pleased.

"It feels as firm as ever," he said, swinging it to and fro. Lissome took the scissors and snipped the cotton.

"Now I'll do the pink cat's tail," she said. The pink cat at once turned round backwards, and Lissome threaded the needle with pink silk to sew on the tail.

Now the blue rabbit had been watching everything with great interest. He couldn't sew – but he did wish he might use those scissors!

Snip, snip, they went, and he wished he could make them go snip, snip, too!

"Let me snip the cotton next time," he begged. So Lissome said he might. He picked up the scissors and put them ready. He snip-snipped them in the air just to practise using them – and then a dreadful thing happened!

He snip-snipped the scissors too near Lissome the elf – and she stepped back just at that moment – and the blue rabbit snipped off one of her lovely wings!

"Oooooh!" cried Lissome in fright. She turned round and saw her lovely wing on the floor. The blue rabbit burst into sobs. He was terribly upset and unhappy.

"Forgive me, forgive me!" he wept. "I didn't mean to. Oh, what shall I do, what shall I do?"

"You wicked, careless rabbit!" cried the pink cat, who saw how pale the elf had gone. "Just when Lissome is doing a kind turn to us you go and snip off one of her beautiful wings!"

"I didn't mean to, I tell you – I didn't mean to!" howled the rabbit, more upset than he had ever been in his life before.

Lissome patted him gently. "Don't cry so," she said. "It was an accident."

"But what will you do?" wept the blue rabbit. "You can't fly now."

"Well, I must just stay in my rose-home until my wing has grown again," said the elf.

"Oh, will it grow again?" cried everyone joyfully. Nobody had thought of that.

"Of course," said the elf. "It will only take a week. So cheer up, Rabbit."

He did cheer up. He squeezed out his wet hanky and tried to smile. Then something else came into his mind, and he looked miserable again.

"*Now* what's the matter?" said the elf.

"I've just thought – you can't fly out of the window tonight," said the rabbit. "So what will you do?"

"Oh, dear," said the elf. "I hadn't thought of that. Can I climb up somehow?"

"No. There's nothing to climb on," said the pink cat. "There's no chair by the window, and we are not big enough to put one there. Rabbit – use your brains. You got Lissome into this muddle. Now get her out of it! Go on – use your brains, if you've got any, or we'll all be very angry with you."

The rabbit thought hard. "We'll hide her!" he said.

"Don't be silly," said the brown bear. "You know that the playroom is turned out tomorrow. There won't be a single corner that isn't swept."

"Put her in the brick-box," said the brown dog.

"Yes – and let Lucy and Jane find her if they use their bricks tomorrow!" said the pink cat scornfully. "And if they treat *us* roughly, what do you suppose they will do to a little elf like Lissome? They would make her *very* unhappy!"

"The brick-box has given me an idea!" said the blue rabbit suddenly. "Let's get all the bricks out – and build a high castle up to the window-sill! Then Lissome can walk up the bricks and climb out to her home!"

"Now that really *is* a good idea!" said the brown bear, and he went to the big brick box. He and the rabbit emptied out the bricks on the floor, and then all the toys began to build a high castle to the window-sill.

It took ages, because the toys were not very good at building, and the bricks kept tumbling down. But at last the castle was done, and just reached the sill!

"It's dawn now!" whispered Lissome, and she climbed up the bricks. "You must sleep, or you will be seen running around. Thank you for your help, Toys! I'll come again when my wing has grown."

The toys heard someone moving about downstairs. Someone was up!

They scuttled into the toy cupboard and shut the door. "We've left the bricks out!" whispered the rabbit, and he lay quite still in a corner. "Oh, dear!"

Well, there wasn't time to put them back into the box, for Lucy and Jane were now both awake and dressing. They rushed into the playroom – and *how* astonished they were to see the bricks leading up to the window-sill!

"Who's built that?" said Lucy.

"And what for?" said Jane.

"The *toys* can't have done it!" said Lucy. "How I'd like to know what it's there for!"

But she never did know. As for the elf, her wing grew again in seven days, and she fluttered in at the window once more, as merry as ever. But she wouldn't let the blue rabbit use the scissors again – and I'm not surprised, are you?

The wallpaper bunnies

On the playroom wall was a lovely wallpaper. It had bunnies all over it. They were nice bunnies, all dressed up in coats and dresses and shawls, and they were doing all kinds of things. Some were shopping, and some were gardening, and some were putting their children to bed.

Ellen and Harry, the two children whose playroom it was, loved their wallpaper. They liked seeing all the bunnies on it, and they knew them very well.

"That's Mrs Flop Bunny going shopping," said Ellen. "And that's Mr Whiskers Bunny who's gardening."

"And that's Mr Woffle Bunny who's

helping him," said Harry. "And those children are the Bobtail Bunnies. I wish they'd all come alive!"

Now the wallpaper bunnies heard the children say this, and at once they began to worry about coming alive. The toys came alive each night. The kitten that played in the playroom was very much alive, and so was Pongo, the dog. Well, why shouldn't the bunnies come alive, too?

So that night, when the toys were all alive-oh, playing catch-me and hide-and-seek in the playroom, the wallpaper bunnies called down to them from the wall.

"Hi, you toys! We want to come alive too!"

The toys stopped their playing and stared at the wallpaper bunnies in surprise. This was the first time they had heard them speak.

"But you can't come alive," they said. "You are only paper."

"Well, what does that matter?" said

Mrs Flop Bunny, from the paper greengrocer's shop! "We can come alive even if we're only paper, can't we? Some of you are only rag and sawdust, but you're alive and kicking!"

"But we don't know how to make you come alive," said the red-haired doll.

"Oh dear! Don't you? Well, we did think that clever toys like you would know how to do that," sighed Mr Woffle Bunny.

The red-haired doll thought hard. Then she spoke to the teddy bear, who nodded his head.

"Well," said the doll, "there's only one thing that I can think of – and that is, we can do what Ellen and Harry do to their paper dolls. We can cut you out of the paper and stand you up! How would you like that?"

"A splendid idea, a truly fine idea!" cried all the wallpaper bunnies, and if they could have moved, they would have danced in delight. But they couldn't.

"I'll borrow the scissors out of the work-basket," said the red-haired doll, getting rather excited.

"Well, mind you put them back, then," said the clockwork clown. "You know how cross Ellen was when I borrowed her thimble for a hat the other night, and forgot to put it back."

The doll went to the work-basket on the chair and opened it. She took out the scissors. She ran over to the wallpaper.

"Snip-snip-snippity-snip!" went her scissors. "Snip-snip-snippity-snip!"

She cut out Mrs Flop Bunny, and her shopping basket too. She cut out Mr Whiskers Bunny and his spade, and Mr Woffle Bunny and his barrow. And she cut out six little Bobtail Bunnies with their hats and shoes and dresses! Really, you should have seen them all!

They hopped down to the playroom floor and scampered about joyfully. What fun it was to be alive!

"I shall do some real shopping!" said Mrs Flop Bunny, and she went to the toy greengrocer's shop that belonged to Harry, and asked the shopman there for three carrots. He put them into her basket, and she was so pleased.

"And I shall really go gardening!" said Mr Whiskers Bunny, and he climbed all the way up the tablecloth with Mr Woffle Bunny and began to dig in the pot of bulbs there! Goodness, wasn't he pleased to see his spade getting nice and earthy! As for Mr Woffle Bunny, he filled his little barrow with real earth and thoroughly enjoyed himself. His barrow felt heavy for the first time.

The Bobtail Bunnies were very frisky. They were only baby bunnies, so they didn't do any work. They just ran about among the toys, who made a great fuss of them.

"Here's a bead necklace for you," said the red-haired doll to a little Bobtail Bunny. She slipped it round the little thing's neck.

"And here's a flower for you," said the teddy bear, taking a daisy out of a vase near by, and giving it to another little Bobtail.

"And here's a brooch for you!" said the clockwork clown, pinning a brooch on to another Bobtail Bunny. The brooch had come out of a cracker, and it was very beautiful.

Well, all the little Bobtail family had presents, and they were all as happy as could be – until something nasty happened.

The Noah's Ark animals had all come out to play – and suddenly the two foxes who lived there saw the wallpaper bunnies! Their eyes gleamed! Rabbits! Aha! They had never had a meal of rabbits – and now here were ever so many scampering all over the playroom!

One Noah's Ark fox hid behind the chair, hoping that a Bobtail Bunny would come by. The other one hid behind the stool.

The toys saw them, and wondered what they were doing. Suddenly the clockwork clown guessed, and he squealed out to the bunnies, "Be careful! The Noah's Ark foxes are out! They may catch you!"

Well, this was a terrible shock to the wallpaper bunnies. There had been no foxes in their wallpaper world, so they really didn't know anything about foxes at all.

Mrs Flop Bunny at once called the Bobtail Bunnies to her, and glared at the fox behind the stool. She could just see his tail.

"How dare you!" she cried. "I won't have you catching the Bobtail children!"

Mr Whiskers Bunny was most alarmed. He put his spade over his shoulder and ran to join Mrs Flop Bunny. As for Mr Woffle Bunny, he tripped over himself and sat down in his barrow of earth! Then, very quickly, he wheeled it off and joined the other bunnies.

The two foxes came out from behind the stool and the chair and stared at the bunnies, their eyes shining, for they were hungry.

"You are *not* to eat the wallpaper bunnies!" said the teddy bear crossly. "Leave them alone."

"We are only made of paper," said Mrs Flop Bunny in a trembling voice. "You would not find us much of a meal. We should probably make you very ill."

"We are really very thin indeed," said Mr Whiskers Bunny, and he turned himself sideways to the foxes, so that they could see he really was as thin as paper. "We may look fat from the front and back, but if you see us sideways we are very narrow indeed."

Just then there was a noise outside the playroom door, and the toys looked alarmed. All the Noah's Ark animals ran to hide, and so did the toys. The Noah's Ark animals hadn't time to get back into the Ark, so some hid in one place and some in another. The two foxes went to hide in the empty brick-box.

Well, it was only a mouse scampering by, after all, so the toys soon got over their fright. Then the clown did something very clever indeed. He ran to the brick-box and put a heavy book on top of it. Now the two foxes inside couldn't get out!

How angry they were! They scrambled round inside that box as if they were chasing bees! But they couldn't get out.

"They're safe for the moment," said the red-haired doll. "But if Ellen or Harry lets them out tomorrow, they'll be after you again the next night, Wallpaper Bunnies. Whatever will you do?"

"It was a great mistake leaving our safe Wallpaper Land," said Mrs Flop Bunny. "There are no foxes there."

"Well, you'd better go back," said the teddy bear.

"We can't," said Mr Whiskers Bunny sorrowfully. "We should fall off the wall if we tried to put ourselves back."

"I know a good idea!" cried the red-haired doll, who really was good at thinking of things. "Where's the glue? You know – that sticky stuff that Ellen uses to stick us together again when we get broken? We could stick the wallpaper bunnies back on the wall again, and nobody would ever know they had left it."

Everybody began to look for the glue. At last it was found. It was in a long tube, and when the teddy bear squeezed one end the glue came out at the other in a sticky worm. It was quite exciting to play with.

The red-haired doll squeezed a little on to the back of every wallpaper bunny. They each took a running jump at the wall, and landed back in their places. The teddy bear fitted them in properly, and the clown smoothed them over with a duster.

Soon they were all back in Wallpaper Land as happy as could be.

"No one will ever know we've been

alive for just one night!" cried Mrs Flop Bunny.

But, you know, Ellen and Harry guessed they had – and do you know why? It was because Mrs Flop Bunny had forgotten to leave behind the three carrots she had put into her basket, which had been empty before! And Mr Whiskers Bunny had forgotten to clean his spade, so it was all dirty; and Mr Woffle Bunny had forgotten to empty out his earth – and as his barrow had been empty before, Ellen and Harry were most puzzled to find it full the next morning!

All the Bobtail Bunnies had their presents with them too, and the children knew quite well they had not worn necklaces and brooches before. It was very mysterious!

"Well, all I can say is that some of the wallpaper bunnies have come alive at some time," said Ellen. "And that's why this little lot look different from how they always used to be. I do wonder why they went back to the wallpaper instead of staying alive?"

They've only got to ask the Noah's Ark foxes and they'll know the reason, won't they?

The quarrelsome bears

There were once two bears who lived in a little yellow cottage in Toy Village. Teddy was a brown bear and Bruiny was a blue one. And how they quarrelled! Really, you should have heard them!

"That's my handkerchief you are using!" said Teddy.

"Indeed it's not!" said Bruiny.

"I tell you it *is*," said Teddy.

"And I tell you it's not!" said Bruiny.

"Don't keep telling me fibs," said Teddy.

"Well, don't you either," said Bruiny.

That was the sort of quarrel they had every single day. Silly, wasn't it? Especially as they both had more handkerchiefs than they needed.

One afternoon they dressed themselves in their best coats and ties to go to a party. They did look nice. Teddy tied Bruiny's bow and Bruiny tied Teddy's. Then they took their new hats and went to the door.

And it was raining! Not just raining quietly, but coming down angrily and fiercely – pitterpatterpitterpatterpitter-patter, without a single stop.

"Goodness! Look at that!" said Teddy. "We must take our umbrella."

They had a big red umbrella between them, and it was really a very fine one indeed. Teddy looked for it in the umbrella-stand. It wasn't there.

"What have you done with the umbrella, Bruiny?" asked Teddy.

"Nothing at all," said Bruiny, at once. "What do you suppose I've done with it? Used it to stir my tea with?"

"Don't be silly," said Teddy. "That umbrella was there yesterday. You must have taken it out."

"I did not," said Bruiny. "You must have taken it yourself."

"I haven't been out for two days," said Teddy. "What do you think I'd want with an umbrella indoors?"

"Oh, you might use it to smack the cat with," said Bruiny unkindly.

"Oh! As if I would smack our dear old cat with an umbrella!" cried Teddy angrily.

"Well – perhaps you used it to poke the fire," said Bruiny.

"And perhaps *you* used it to scrub the floor!" cried Teddy. "I can think of silly things too. No, it's no good, Bruiny. You took that umbrella for something, and you might just as well try and remember what you did with it and where you put it. Hurry, now, or we'll be late for the party."

"I tell you, Teddy, I haven't had the umbrella and I don't know where it is," said Bruiny. "It would be a good thing if *you* thought a little and found out where you had hidden it."

"I don't hide umbrellas," said Teddy.

"Well, you once hid the cat in the cupboard and it jumped out at me," said Bruiny.

"That was just a joke," said Teddy. "I shouldn't hide our umbrella in the cupboard, because it wouldn't jump out at you."

"But you'd like it to, I suppose?" cried Bruiny, getting crosser and crosser.

"Yes, I'd love to see an umbrella jump out at you!" shouted Teddy, getting angry too.

"You're a bad teddy bear!" said Bruiny, and he pulled Teddy's bow undone.

"Don't!" cried Teddy. He caught hold of Bruiny's coat, meaning to give him a good shaking. But he shook too hard and the coat tore in half!

"Oh! Oh! Look at that!" wailed Bruiny. "I'll jump on your hat for tearing my coat!"

And before Teddy could stop him, Bruiny had thrown his new hat on the floor and jumped on it. It was quite spoilt!

Then they both went mad. They tore each other's ties off. They threw both hats out of the window. They even threw each other's handkerchiefs into the waste-paper basket!

And in the middle of all this there came a knocking at the door! Bruiny went to open it, panting and torn. Outside stood Mrs Field-Mouse with all her little family. They were on their way to the party, each mouse under its own tiny umbrella.

"Goodness me! What's all the noise about?" asked Mrs Field-Mouse severely. "I knocked three times before you heard me."

"Well, Mrs Field-Mouse," said Bruiny, "Teddy has taken our umbrella and doesn't know where he put it."

"Oh, you fibber!" cried Teddy. "It's Bruiny that must have taken it, Mrs Field-Mouse. We've only got one, and it's raining, and we wanted it to go to the party."

"Dear me!" said Mrs Field-Mouse.

"What have *you* come for?" asked Bruiny.

"Well, I came to give you back your big red umbrella," said Mrs Field-Mouse with a laugh. "I suppose you forgot that you both kindly said I might have it yesterday to go home with my little family, because it was big enough to shelter them all. I promised to bring it back today. Here it is. I'm sorry you should have quarrelled about it."

She stood it in the hall-stand and then went off to the party with her little family. How they squealed when they heard the joke!

"Well, I never," said Bruiny, looking at the umbrella. "So you didn't take it, Teddy."

"And you didn't either," said Teddy. "Oh dear, how silly we are! We've got our umbrella – but we've torn our suits and ties and spoilt our hats, so we can't possibly go to the party after all."

"I beg your pardon, Teddy," said Bruiny in a small voice. "I'll make you some cocoa for tea."

"And I beg your pardon, too," said Teddy. "I'll make you some toast for tea. We'll never quarrel again!"

But they did quarrel, and do you know why? It was because Teddy couldn't find the toasting-fork, so he toasted the bread on the end of the red umbrella! Bruiny was so angry, because he said the toast tasted of mud!

Well, well, well! You can't please everybody, can you?

The six fairy dolls

In the toyshop sat six fairy dolls. They were all sizes. The biggest was nearly two feet high, and very lovely. The next was smaller, and the third and fourth were pretty little dolls with silvery wings. The fifth one was only six inches high, but she was beautifully dressed, and carried a silver wand.

The last one was very tiny, and stood no higher than a child's little finger. Her wings were only silver paper, and her wand was a bit of wire. Her dress was the tiniest bit of muslin, and her feet were so small that she wore no shoes at all.

The big dolls talked together, and didn't take any notice of the tiny fairy

doll. She listened to them, and wished she was as big as they were.

“We are sure to be bought for a Christmas party,” said one fairy doll. “I am the biggest, so I expect I shall be chosen first. I shall be put right at the top of a big Christmas tree, and I shall be able to look down and see everything.”

“I am nearly as big as you,” said the second. “I expect I shall be bought too. I would do nicely for a smaller Christmas tree.”

“We are very pretty little dolls,” said the third and fourth. “We heard the shopkeeper say so when she put us in the window. She said we were sure to sell.”

“I am the prettiest of you all,” said the fifth. “I have the loveliest dress – it is all made by hand – and my wand glitters just like silver! I am very grand. I expect I shall be bought by a very rich lady for her children’s tree. I shall go first, I am sure.”

"What about me?" asked the tiniest doll. "Shall I be bought too?"

"Pooh, you!" said all the other dolls at once. "There's no Christmas tree small enough for you! You'll never be sold. You'll just stay on the shelf for years, and then get so dirty that you'll have to be thrown away."

The days went past, and Christmas came near. No one came to buy any of the fairy dolls at all. They were very much disappointed. At last Christmas Eve came, and just as the shopkeeper was going to close the shop for the night, the shop bell tinkled.

All the fairy dolls sat up straight. Perhaps someone was going to buy them at last! It was a little old woman, and she looked across to the fairy dolls.

"I want a fairy doll, please," she said. The shopkeeper fetched them all and sat them on the counter.

"How lovely they are!" said the little old woman. "But most of them are much too big. I want just a little tiny one to put on a Christmas cake."

"Then this one would be just right," said the shopkeeper, and she took up the tiniest doll of all. How proud and pleased she was!

"Yes, that one will do nicely!" said the old woman. She put a ten pence piece down on the counter, and the shopkeeper wrapped the little doll in brown paper. All the other dolls stared in dismay. The tiny doll had been bought first, after all. No one had wanted *them*! What a disappointment!

"We'd better not be so proud of ourselves next Christmas!" whispered the biggest fairy doll, as the shopkeeper packed them away in boxes for the next year. "I wonder what that tiny little doll is doing now?"

Ah, she was having a fine time! She had been put right in the very middle of a beautiful Christmas cake. Round her were little brown bunnies and little red gnomes made of marzipan. They thought the fairy doll was the most beautiful thing they had ever seen.

"You shall be our little queen!" they said. And at midnight they crowned her, and danced round her in a ring. How happy she was! When tea-time came on Christmas Day everyone admired her, and all the children said how sweet she was. They begged their mother to be careful not to cut her when she cut the cake.

And what became of her after the party? Well, she was put into the dolls' house to look after it! She is just the right size, and you may be sure she keeps the house beautifully! There isn't a speck of dust anywhere. She sleeps in the little bed there every night, and is as happy as a lark in spring-time. You should just hear her singing when she cooks her breakfast on the little tin stove in the dolls' house kitchen!

The bear with button eyes

There was once a little teddy bear who had button eyes. He could see quite well with them, but he couldn't shut them to go to sleep. He didn't mind this a bit because he was always very wide awake.

Now one day, Mollie, his little mistress, took him out into the garden to play, and suddenly a dreadful thing happened. One of his button eyes came loose, and dropped into the grass! How upset the little bear was!

Mollie didn't notice it. She was setting out her tea set, and didn't see that the bear had only one eye. He did his best to show her, but she went on playing tea-parties, and didn't look at him.

"Oh my, oh my!" thought the little bear, "what am I to do? I am going to a dance with all the other toys tonight, and I can't go with only one eye!"

Then Mollie heard her mother calling her to come in and she quickly put her toys away and ran indoors, taking the teddy with her. The bear couldn't think *what* he was to do! He really *must* get his eye back before the dance that night!

He sat in the toy cupboard, very sad and quiet. His friend the bunny-rabbit wondered what was the matter.

"What is making you so sad?" he asked, putting a soft paw into the teddy bear's brown one.

"One of my button eyes fell out on to the grass," said the bear, sadly. "Mollie didn't notice, and I am sure I don't know how I can go to a dance with only one eye. What am I to do?"

The bunny thought hard. Then he squeezed the bear's paw.

"As soon as it is night and the moon

is up, I will take all the toy soldiers into the garden and they shall look for your button eye," he said.

"Oh, thank you," said the bear, very gratefully.

So as soon as Mollie had gone to bed, and the moon was up, the bunny-rabbit made all the toy soldiers march out of their fortress and follow him into the garden. Then they looked and looked and looked for the button eye.

But they couldn't find it! It was most surprising. It wasn't anywhere in the garden at all.

A little brownie came running by, and he stopped in astonishment to see so many toy soldiers about.

"Whatever are you doing here?" he asked.

"Looking for teddy bear's button eye," said the rabbit. "He dropped it here this afternoon, and he says he can't go to our dance tonight without it."

"Good gracious!" said the brownie. "I

know what has happened to it!"

"What?" asked all the soldiers and the bunny together.

"Why, Fairy Littlefeet came by this evening," said the brownie, "and she had lost a black button from her right shoe. Suddenly she saw one in the grass, and she picked it up and sewed it on to her shoe. I lent her a needle and thread myself."

"Oh my!" said the bunny in dismay. "Now what are we to do? Do you know where Littlefeet lives?"

"No," said the brownie. "I don't. I'm afraid the bear won't get his button eye back now."

Everyone was quite quiet, thinking what to do. Then at last the brownie spoke.

"If only you could get another button from somewhere, I could perhaps sew it on for you myself," he said.

The bunny thanked him very much.

"There may be one in Mollie's work-basket," he said. "I'll go and see."

So he and all the soldiers went back into the playroom again and hunted in Mollie's work-basket. But there were only pearl buttons there, and those wouldn't do for eyes. The bunny was in despair. What could he do for the teddy bear? It was getting nearly time to start the dance, and he did so badly want his friend to go.

Then he thought of a splendid idea. He knew that Mollie wore shoes with buttons on. If only he could find those, perhaps he could cut one off, and that would do splendidly for the bear.

So he hurried to the boot cupboard. But Mollie's black shoes had gone to be mended, and there was only a white pair there, with white buttons on.

"Perhaps a white button would do just as well," thought the bunny. "I expect he could see with it all right."

So he took a pair of scissors and snipped the button from one shoe. Then he ran to the bear.

"Come along," he said. "I've got a button that will do for you. It's white, but I'm sure it won't matter."

He took him to the brownie, and the little man fetched a reel of spider thread and a pine needle. In a trice he had sewn on the white boot button, and the teddy bear had two eyes!

"I can see beautifully!" he said, looking all round. "That is splendid! Do I look very funny?"

He did look a bit odd with one white eye and one black one, but the bunny told him that he looked lovely. So off he went to the dance feeling very happy.

Now in the morning Mollie went to put her white shoes on – and wasn't she surprised to find the button gone!

"Why, both buttons were there when I put them away yesterday," she said. "Where can the other one be?"

Then she suddenly caught sight of the teddy bear, staring at her with his one black button eye and his one white one. She ran to him and picked him up.

"Oh, you poor darling!" she cried. "How did you get that white button for an eye? You had two black ones yesterday! The fairies must have come in the night and sewn it on for you!"

Mollie looked at it carefully and saw that it was most beautifully sewn on with spider thread instead of cotton. Then she knew for certain that some fairy had been at work, and she was filled with delight.

"Now I know there are fairies!" she cried. "Oh, Teddy, you shall keep your white eye to remind me. I do wish you could tell me what had happened!"

But he never did tell her. He still has one white and one black button for eyes, so if ever you meet him you are sure to know him!

The rabbit who lost his tail

In the playroom cupboard with all the other toys lived Bun the soft rabbit. He was dressed in an orange tunic and green shorts, and his tail stuck out behind. It was a funny little tail, very short and fluffy, just like a real rabbit's.

Bun often played with Mollie, his mistress. She used to take him into the garden with her, and he sat on a little wooden chair and pretended to have tea. He was a very happy little rabbit.

One day a pixie climbed in at the window and gave Bun a letter. It had a crown printed on the back, so Bun knew that it had come from a King or Queen. He was very excited and his

paws trembled when they tried to undo the envelope.

All the other toys crowded round to see what the letter inside was. Bun unfolded it and read it out loud. It was from the King of Fairyland!

DEAR BUN,
I am having a party under the old beech tree on Wednesday night at moonrise. Please come if you can.
Love from
THE KING OF FAIRYLAND.

Bun danced for joy. He had always wanted to go to a pixie party, but toys didn't very often get asked.

"Wednesday!" he said. "That's two days away. Oh, how can I wait?"

Bun was very happy all that day – but the next day something dreadful happened. He lost his tail!

Mollie had taken him out into the garden to play with him and the little boy next door came to play too. But he was rather rough with Bun, and to make Mollie laugh he held the little rabbit up by his tail.

But Mollie didn't laugh. She snatched Bun away from the little boy and scolded him.

"That's not funny!" she said. "You'll hurt Bun. You're a nasty little boy and I don't want to play with you any more."

Then the two began to quarrel, and soon they were shouting at each other loudly. Mother came out and sent the little boy away. Then she took Mollie indoors.

All that day Bun lay out on the grass. The rain came and made him wet. Then suddenly Mollie remembered him and ran out to fetch him. She sat him in front of the playroom fire to dry, and there he stayed in the warm until Mollie went to bed.

Then, when the playroom was empty and quiet, all the other toys crept round Bun to hear what had happened. He told them all about the little boy who held him up by the tail and the toys exclaimed in horror.

Then suddenly the bear gave a squeak.

"Ooh, Bun!" he said. "Where *is* your tail?"

Then all the toys looked at Bun's back, and sure enough his tail was gone. He had no tail at all.

He *was* upset! He turned his head round to look at the place where his tail wasn't, and the tears came into his eyes.

"What shall I do?" he wept. "I can't go to a pixie party without a tail, I really can't. Why, I should feel only half-dressed. Oh, whatever shall I do?"

The toys looked at one another and thought hard.

"I'll run out into the garden and see if I can find your tail for you," said the clockwork clown. "If someone will wind me up, I can easily get there and back."

The teddy bear wound him up and the clockwork clown ran out of the room and down the passage that led to the garden. He hunted everywhere about the grass for Bun's tail, but he couldn't find it. At last he didn't dare to hunt any longer for he was afraid his clockwork would run down, and then he wouldn't be able to get back to the playroom.

"Well," said the toys, when he went back to them, "did you find it?"

"No," said the clown, "it isn't there."

Then Bun wept more loudly than ever, and all the toys looked at one another and thought hard again.

"Couldn't one of you lend me a tail?" asked Bun, at last.

"I haven't got one or I would with pleasure," said the teddy bear.

"What about the baby lamb that lives in the toy stable?" cried the clown. "He has a fine long tail, and I am sure he would lend it to you."

"But wouldn't I look funny with a very long tail?" asked Bun. "My own was so short."

"Oh, a long tail is better than nothing," said the teddy, and all the toys agreed. So they went to fetch the baby lamb from the stable and told him what they wanted. He didn't like parting with his tail at first, but when the clown told him all about the wonderful pixie party that Bun had been invited to, he said yes, he would lend his tail just for that night.

"It's only pinned on," he said, "so Bun can quite easily unpin it and put it on himself."

"Well, I'll borrow it tomorrow, and thank you very much," said Bun, happily. Then all the toys went to sleep, and the playroom was quiet.

The next night the toys fetched the lamb again, and the clown unpinned his tail. It was very long, soft and woolly and felt lovely and warm. Bun turned his back to the clown, and in a trice it was neatly pinned on.

"Ooh, Bun!" said the teddy bear, "you do look fine! A long tail suits you much better than a short one. Everyone will look at you and admire you."

Bun felt very happy. He took his invitation card, said goodbye to the toys and set off to the big beech tree. The moon was just rising, and as he came near the tree he could see crowds of pixies and elves there.

Bun wondered if Tiptoe, the elf who lived in the foxglove bed, was going to the party too. He was very fond of Tiptoe, and he had often wished that she would marry him and live with him in the playroom. But he had never dared to ask her, for she was very lovely.

Suddenly he saw her. She ran up to him and tweaked one of his big ears.

"Hello, Bun!" she said. "I'm so glad you're going to the party."

"Will you dance with me?" asked Bun, in delight.

"Yes," said Tiptoe, and then she sneezed three times.

"Oh dear, you haven't got a cold, have you?" asked Bun in alarm. "What a thin dress you have on, Tiptoe, and the wind is so cold too."

"Yes, I ought to have put on something warmer," said Tiptoe, and she shivered, "but it's too late now. Perhaps I shall get warm dancing."

The party soon began. The band struck up a merry tune, and all the pixies and elves began to dance. The King and Queen sat on two toadstool thrones, and clapped when each dance was finished.

Bun enjoyed himself very much, because everyone admired his tail.

"What a beautiful tail!" they said. "You *are* a lucky rabbit to have a tail like that! How nice you look! Will you dance with us?"

So Bun danced every single dance, and was so happy that his ears turned bright red inside. But he liked dancing best with Tiptoe. He was worried about her because she did sneeze so, and he

felt certain she would get a very bad cold, and be ill.

Suddenly the Queen heard Tiptoe sneezing and she called her to the throne.

"Why didn't you put on a warmer dress?" she said. "You really must go home, Tiptoe, for you will get a terrible cold."

"Oh, please, Your Majesty, do let me stay!" said poor Tiptoe. "A-tishoo, a-tishoo!"

Then a wonderful idea came to Bun. He ran up to the Queen and bowed.

"I can lend Tiptoe a fur to put round her neck," he said. "Would you let her stay if she wears a fur, Your Majesty?"

"Certainly," said the Queen. "But where is the fur?"

"Here!" said Bun, and he unpinned the long woolly lamb's tail! He put it around Tiptoe's neck, and there she was, as warm as toast, and as pretty as a picture.

How all the elves and pixies cheered! They knew that Bun was proud of his long tail and felt very odd without it, and they thought it was very kind and unselfish of him to lend it to Tiptoe and go without it himself.

After that Bun was more of a hero than ever. All the elves wanted to dance with him, but he danced all the rest of the time with Tiptoe, who had stopped sneezing and felt quite warm with the lamb's tail round her neck.

"I'll see you home," said Bun, after the party. "You can wear the fur all the way to the foxglove bed, and when you're nice and warm at home, you can give me the tail to take back to the baby lamb, who lent it to me. I lost my own tail."

"How sad for you!" said Tiptoe. "But what a good thing for me, because if you hadn't lost your own tail you wouldn't have been able to lend me this fur, and I should have had to go home early! Tomorrow I'll have a good hunt for your own tail, Bun. Now, goodnight, and thank you for your kindness."

Bun said goodnight and ran home very happy. He told all the toys what had happened and the baby lamb was very pleased when he heard how useful his tail had been. The teddy bear pinned it on to his back again, and then all the toys settled themselves to sleep.

Next evening there came a tapping at the playroom window and who should it be but Tiptoe!

"Bun!" she called. "Bun! Come quickly! I've found your tail!"

Bun ran to the window and opened it. There was Tiptoe, and in her hand was Bun's own little short tail.

"Where did you find it?" he asked, in delight.

"A worm had pulled it down into his hole," said Tiptoe. "I took it away from him and washed it. Now it is dry and clean, and if you come with me I'll sew it on so tightly for you that you will never lose it again."

So Bun went to the foxglove bed with Tiptoe and she sewed his tail on for him again with a hundred stitches so that it was very firm indeed.

"You are the dearest elf I ever saw!" said Bun. "I do wish you would marry me, Tiptoe. We could live in the dolls' house, and be very happy together."

"Ooh, let's!" said Tiptoe, and she flung her arms round Bun and hugged him. He had never been so happy in all his life.

They moved into the dolls' house, and, oh, what a merry time they had! They gave parties every night, and Tiptoe learnt to cook lovely cakes on the little tin stove in the kitchen. And they *always* ask the baby lamb to their parties, because if it hadn't been for his long woolly tail Bun and Tiptoe would never have got married!

The tale of a tail

A most exciting letter had come from the brownies in the wood to the toys in Michael's playroom. This is what it said.

"Dear Animals,

We are holding a party for all toy animals in the woods at midnight tomorrow. Please come.

Love from

The Brownies.

PS – By animals we mean those with tails."

"Oh! A party in the woods just for toy animals! What a wonderful idea," said the clockwork mouse.

"I shall wear my best blue bow," said the pink cat.

"I shall put a special wag in my tail," said the black dog.

"I shall practise climbing so that I can climb the trees," said the monkey.

"And I shall make sure my growl is in good order, so that I can make the brownies laugh," said the teddy bear.

The pink cat looked at him. "You can't go to the party," she said.

"Don't be silly," said the bear. "Of course I can go. I'm an animal! Bears are always animals."

"Yes, but you haven't got a tail," said the pink cat. "You saw what it said in the note. 'By animals we mean those with tails.' "

The bear stared behind him in alarm. "Haven't I got a tail?" he said. "Why haven't I got a tail?"

"I don't know, I don't believe teddy bears ever have tails," said the pink cat. "Anyway, you can't go. It plainly says that only those with tails can go."

"But it didn't mean *I* can't go," said the bear. "Why, everyone knows I'm an animal! I can't help it if I haven't got a tail. It just means that people like the baby doll or the sailor doll can't go. It doesn't mean bears."

"Well, I'm sure it *does*," said the black dog. "They think you're a toy, like the baby doll. They don't count you as an animal. You can't possibly go, Teddy. They might turn you back."

The bear began to cry. He did like parties so very much. "Oh, don't go without me! I couldn't bear it," he sobbed. "Please, please let me go with you. Don't go without me."

The toys were sorry for him. He was a nice bear, kind and jolly. It was a shame he couldn't go because he had no tail.

Then the monkey had an idea. "I know! Can't he get a tail? Then he could go!"

"Oh, yes, oh, yes! I'll get a tail!" cried the bear, and wiped his eyes at once. He gave the monkey a hug. "How kind of you to think of such a good idea! Where can I get a tail?"

Nobody knew. Then the black dog remembered something he had heard Michael say. Michael was the little boy who lived in the house and played with the toys.

"I once heard Michael say that his favourite tail was in that book over there," he said, and he pointed to a book on the bookshelf. The toys stared in surprise.

"I didn't know Michael had a tail," said the bear.

"He hasn't," said the toy boat. "I swim in the bath with him, and I know he hasn't got a tail. He has a dear little pink fat body, but no tail."

"Well, he keeps it in that book, I tell you," said the black dog. "He must have two or three tails, and that is his favourite one, the one in the book."

"Are you *sure* you heard him say his favourite tail was in the book?" said the monkey.

"Yes. Quite, quite sure," said the black dog, impatiently. "I've got two good ears, haven't I?"

"Well, then, we've only got to look through the book and borrow the tail when we find it," said the pink cat. "I should think it would be a bit squashed, but that won't matter."

So they got the book down and began to hunt through it. But they couldn't find any tail at all. And this wasn't surprising, because what Michael had meant, of course, was that his favourite story or *tale* was in that book – but the black dog had quite thought he meant a waggy tail, like the one he wore himself.

It was very disappointing. There was no tail there at all. They turned all the pages over again very carefully. Still no tail.

"Michael must have taken it out," said the monkey. The bear looked very sad. He rubbed his paw over his eyes, and the curly-haired doll gave him her hanky.

"Don't cry," she said. "Maybe Michael has put it somewhere else. We'll look."

But they couldn't find a tail anywhere, of course. The bear was very sad that night, and very sad all the next day.

When the night of the party came he was sadder still. It would be dreadful to watch the toys going off to the party without him. If only, only he had a tail.

Then he would be counted as an animal.

"Shall we set the musical box going, just to practise a dance or two before we go?" said the monkey. "I've rather forgotten my dance steps."

So they set the musical box going, and began to dance. The bear stood near, watching sadly. If only he was going to dance at a party too!

The toys had forgotten to shut the door, and Michael awoke when he heard the music from the musical box. He sat up in bed in surprise. Who was playing the musical box in the middle of the night?

He jumped out of bed to see. He put his head in at the playroom door, and watched the toy animals dancing together. The monkey danced with the dog. The cat danced with the toy horse. The donkey danced with the mouse. The rabbit danced with the little toy lamb.

Only the bear didn't dance. He stood near the door, his back to Michael, and tears ran down his face. He turned away to hide them – and Michael saw that his dear old teddy was crying.

"What's the matter?" he said to the bear, and all the toys and animals jumped in great surprise. They shot back into the toy cupboard at top speed. Only the bear stayed where he was, and looked at Michael.

"Why are you crying, Teddy?" said Michael, and picked up the fat, little bear. "I've never seen you cry before. I didn't know you could."

"Michael – you said your favourite tail was in that book, but it isn't," said the bear. "Where do you keep your tails? Could you lend me one?"

Michael couldn't understand at first. Then he guessed the funny mistake that the bear had made and he laughed. "You've muddled up what I meant!" he said. "I meant that my favourite story was in that book, silly! I have no tail – not the sort that grow on you."

"Oh, dear," said the bear, sadly. "I see.

So you can't lend me one. And I can't possibly go to the party."

"What party?" asked Michael, surprised. The bear told him all about it.

"Well, fancy saying that only animals with tails can go! I'm sure that's a mistake," said Michael. "But never mind – let's see what I can find for you in the way of a tail. I'm sure I can think of something."

He remembered an old hat of his mother's. It had a little tail of white fur in front. He could take that off and sew it on the bear! That would make a most wonderful tail for him.

Michael went to find the old hat. It was in a box in the chest on the landing. Mother had often said she didn't think she could ever wear it again. Michael took it out – and there was the little white tail, just as he remembered it. Good!

He ripped it off. Then he found a needle and cotton in his mother's work-basket and he threaded the needle.

"Shall I hurt you if I sew this on your back?" he asked the bear.

"Oh no," said the bear. "What a simply lovely tail! It looks so real! Shall I be able to wag it?"

"I don't know," said Michael, feeling rather doubtful. "It hasn't a wag in it at the moment. Now, keep still. It doesn't match your brown fur, but never mind!"

He sewed the white tail firmly on to the bear's back. He broke off the cotton and gave the bear a little push. "There you are! Turn round and show the others. You look really fine!"

The bear was so proud that he couldn't stand still. He strutted up and down, showing off his grand white tail. It was a bit big for him and didn't match. But he was so very happy about it. His happiness suddenly got into the tail, and it began to swing about.

"It's got a wag! Look, it's got a wag!" said the bear, happily, and he swung his new tail so well that he hit the clockwork mouse on the nose.

"It's time to start," said the black cat, as he heard the clock in the hall strike a quarter to twelve. "Goodbye, Michael. Thank you for your help."

"Have a nice time!" said Michael, and went back to bed, delighted at his little midnight adventure.

The animals all set off to the party. The bear didn't feel a bit afraid of being turned back now that he had a tail. He swung it about all the time.

To his surprise there were other teddy bears there – without tails! The brownies explained their mistake, and welcomed all the bears that came.

"We forgot that teddy bears didn't have tails. We are so glad you came."

"*Well*! I needn't have gone to all this bother of getting myself a tail after all!" said the bear, feeling rather cross.

But he didn't feel cross for long. You see, there was a special prize offered for the best tail – and the teddy bear won it! His was such a big and surprising tail that everyone voted it was the very best one. So he got the prize.

It was a fine prize. It was a box of chocolates – and each chocolate was a little brown bear! Wasn't that lovely? The bear ate one and handed the box round.

"I must keep a few for Michael," he thought. "I really must." So he did. He put them on Michael's pillow, and Michael found them in the morning.

"I suppose the bear brought them home for me from the party," thought Michael, eating them. "How kind of him! I must take his tail off today and put it back on Mummy's hat."

But the bear didn't want to part with his beautiful new tail, so Michael asked his mother if she minded him keeping the tail off her old hat. She didn't, so Michael let the bear keep it.

He still wears it, so you will know him if you ever see him. He must be the only teddy bear in the world with a tail!

It's Christmas time

"It's Christmas time!" said the big rocking-horse in the toy shop, one night when the shop was shut, and only the light of the street lamp outside lit up the toys sitting on the shelves and counters.

"What's Christmas?" asked a small bear who had only just come.

"Oh, it's a lovely time for children," said the horse, rocking gently to and fro. "They have presents, you know, and Father Christmas comes on Christmas night and fills their stockings with all kinds of toys."

"*You'll* never go into a stocking, rocking-horse!" said a cheeky monkey.

"No, I shall stand in somebody's

playroom and give children rides," said the horse. "I *shall* look forward to that. I've been here a long time – too long. But I'm very expensive, you know, and people often haven't enough money to buy me."

"I should like to be sold and go to live with children who would love me and play with me," said the fat teddy bear. "I shall growl for them – listen – urrrrrrrr-rrrrr!"

"Don't!" said the little furry rabbit sitting next to him. "You frighten me when you do that. I think you're going to bite me."

"Don't worry. You know he wouldn't," said the big sailor doll, leaning down from the shelf above. "Come on, Bunny – let's get down to the floor and have a game!"

The rabbit jumped down at once, and the big sailor doll landed near him. He loved the sailor, who wouldn't let any of the bigger toys tease him or frighten him. Sometimes the pink cat chased him and the little rabbit couldn't bear that!

"Sailor," said the rabbit, when all the toys were playing together, "Sailor, we're friends, aren't we? Sailor, you won't leave me if you are sold and go to live with some children, will you?"

"Well – I shan't be able to help it," said Sailor. "You're my very best friend and I'm yours, and I hope and hope we'll be sold together – but you never know!"

The bunny worried about that, and next day when customers came in and out of the shop, buying this toy and that, the little rabbit hoped that he and the sailor doll would be bought by the same person.

But they weren't! A little old woman came in and asked for a sailor doll for her grand-daughter whose father was a sailor – and the shop lady at once took down Sailor from his shelf.

"He's fine," said the little old woman. "Yes, I'll have him. My grand-daughter Mary will love him! Will you wrap him up for me, please?"

"Goodbye, Sailor!" whispered the little rabbit. "Oh, I shall miss you so! Goodbye, and be happy!"

Sailor only had time to wave before he was wrapped up in brown paper. Then he was carried out of the shop by the old woman, and Bunny was left by himself. He felt lonely and unhappy, and he hoped that the bear wouldn't growl at him or the pink cat chase him.

But he was sold that very day too! A big, smiling woman came in and bought a great many toys at once.

"They're for a Christmas tree," she said. "I am giving a party on Boxing Day for my little girl and her friends, and we've got a perfectly lovely tree."

"You'll want a fairy doll for the top, then," said the shop lady, pleased. "And what about a little bear and a doll or two?"

"Yes. And I'll have that ship – and that wooden engine – and that top," said the customer. "And I really *must* have that little rabbit – he's sweet!"

Bunny was sold! He couldn't believe it. He was sold at last and would leave the toy shop he knew so well. He was glad he was going with so many other toys he knew – but oh dear, each of them would be given to a different child, so he wouldn't have any friends at all after Boxing Day!

The toys were excited. It was fun to be sold and to go out to some family. It would be fun to hang on a Christmas tree and have crowds of children admiring them. It would be simply lovely if they were lucky enough to belong to a kind and loving child who would play with them and perhaps even cuddle them in bed.

Bunny was surprised to see such a big Christmas tree. It almost reached the ceiling! "I don't think I want to be hung up there," he said to the big teddy bear, who had been sold for the tree too. "I might fall off."

"Don't be silly," said the bear. "Ah – here comes someone to see to us! Cheer up, you silly little rabbit, and if you are given to some horrid child, well, just run away!"

"Where to?" asked the rabbit, anxiously, but the bear was very busy growling at that moment, because someone was pressing him in the middle where his growl was kept!

"Urrrr!" he said proudly. "Urrrr!"

The rabbit was hung high up on the tree, and dangled to and fro there. He didn't like it. The ground seemed so far away! All the other toys hung there too, and pretty fairylights shone brightly in red, blue, yellow and green from the top of the tree to the bottom.

"The party's tonight!" said a doll next to him. "Not long to wait now! Doesn't the fairy doll look wonderful at the top of the tree?"

Soon the rabbit heard the sound of children's voices and laughter. They were playing games in another room.

Then someone came quickly into the big room where the tree stood and switched on all the fairylights again. The tree glowed and shone, and all the pretty ornaments on it glittered brightly. The toys looked lovely as they hung there.

How the children cheered and clapped when they came running in and saw the lovely tree. "It's beautiful!" they shouted. "Oh, look at the toys! Oh, the fairy doll! Wave your wand, fairy doll, and do some magic!"

"Now, there is a toy for everyone," said the lady who was giving the party. "Harry, here is a ship for you," and she gave him the ship. "Lucy, here is a doll. I know you want one. Molly, here is a bear with a growl."

The little rabbit looked down on the children. Was there a little girl called Mary there? The sailor doll had been bought for a Mary. Oh, wouldn't it be wonderful if he was given to a girl called Mary, the one who had Sailor?

Who was Bunny going to? He looked and looked at the children. He did hope somebody kind would have him – a nice little girl, perhaps, with a merry face.

"And now, what about a present for *you*, Peter," said the kind lady at the tree. "You're not very old – I think you shall have this little furry bunny. Here you are!"

So Bunny went to Peter, who held him very tight indeed, and squeezed him to see if he had a squeak inside. But he hadn't. Bunny didn't like Peter very much, especially when he dropped him on the floor and somebody nearly trod on him.

"Be careful of your little rabbit, Peter," said a big girl.

"I don't like him," said Peter. "I wanted that engine."

The rabbit wondered if he could run away. He didn't want to go home with Peter. He was sure he was one of the horrid children he had heard spoken about in the toy shop.

But he did go home with Peter, and with him went a jigsaw puzzle for Peter's sister.

"Give this to your sister, Peter," said somebody. "It is such a pity she's in bed with a cold and can't come. This jigsaw shall be her present."

Peter carried the rabbit and the jigsaw home. As soon as he got there he went up to his sister's bedroom. She was in bed, with a large hanky under her pillow.

"Look – they sent you a jigsaw," said Peter. "And I got this silly little rabbit. I'd much rather have the jigsaw!"

"Oh, Peter – he's sweet!" said the little girl in bed. "I've so many jigsaws – you take that one and I'll have the bunny. He shall come into bed with me, he looks rather lonely. He's only a baby one!"

"All right. I'd like the jigsaw," said Peter. He threw the rabbit to his sister and went out with the jigsaw. The little girl took the rabbit and looked at him. "Yes, I like you," she said. "You shall sleep with me at night, so long as you don't mind sharing my bed with another toy. Look, here he is – my very best new toy!"

She pulled back the sheet – and Bunny stared as if he couldn't believe his eyes. Who do you suppose was cuddled down in bed, looking very happy? Why, Sailor! Yes, it was the big sailor doll, the one from the toy shop, Bunny's own special friend. Sailor almost sat up in surprise, but just remembered not to. He smiled, though, he smiled and smiled!

"I think you like each other," said Mary, because that was her name, of course! "Yes, I'm sure you do. I hope so, anyway, because you've just *got* to be friends. You see, you will sit together on my bed each day, and cuddle down with me at night!" She put Bunny beside Sailor, and lay down. She closed her eyes, and was soon asleep. And then – what a whispering there was beside her!

"*You!*" said Sailor, in delight. "What a bit of luck!"

"*You!*" said Bunny. "Oh, I can't believe it! What's Mary like?"

"Fine," said Sailor. "You'll love her. Oh, Bun – what lovely times we're going to have! You'll like the other toys here, too, all except a rude monkey – but I won't let him tease you! Fancy, we shall be able to be friends all our lives now!"

That was three years ago – and they are still with Mary, though they don't sleep with her at night now, because she thinks she's too big for that. "It *is* nice to have a friend," Bun keeps saying. Well, it is, isn't it?

Magic in the playroom

The toys in the playroom were very friendly with the little folk who lived in the garden. There were fairies and pixies, gnomes and brownies, all merry and happy and friendly. Sometimes it was the gnomes who came to drink a cup of tea in the dolls' house. Sometimes it was the pixies who came to dance to the music of the little musical box. And sometimes it was the fairies or the brownies who came to play at hide-and-seek with the toys.

They did have fun, and the toys always loved to see the pretty heads of the little folk peeping over the window-sill. But when a family of goblins came to live in the old oak tree in the garden the toys were not quite so pleased to see them.

"The goblins are not so polite as the fairies," said the pink rabbit, shaking his head.

"The goblins have rather bad

manners," said the big doll.

"They make a noise when they eat," said the red-haired doll, who was very particular indeed.

But nobody said anything rude to the goblins, and each night they popped in at the window with the other little folk.

Then a horrid thing happened. One night, after the little folk had gone back to the garden, the pink rabbit put his hand up to his collar and found that the little brooch which kept his coat together at the neck was quite gone!

"I believe I saw it peeping out of the pocket of one of the goblins," said the clockwork mouse suddenly.

There was a deep silence. The toys were too shocked for words. To think that one of their guests would steal something!

"You must be wrong, Mouse," said the pink rabbit at last. "My brooch must have dropped somewhere."

So they hunted for it, but it could not

be found. "We will not say anything about it at all," said the rabbit. "It is horrid to think that anyone would steal from us."

But after that other things began to go! The red-haired doll missed her necklace! She usually kept it in the kitchen cupboard in the dolls' house, because she was so afraid of losing it – and one night when she went to put it on, it was not in the cupboard! Oh dear!

And worse than that, the walking duck lost her key! It was always kept on a ribbon, tied to her neck, so that it should not be lost. It was easy to wind up the walking duck when she had her key handy like that. But now it was gone! Someone had cut her ribbon in half and taken the key, perhaps when she was playing a game and was too excited to notice.

The toys stared at one another in dismay. Something really *must* be done now! There was no doubt at all that those bad-tempered little goblins had taken their things.

"We will complain to the others," said the walking duck. "Surely the fairies, the pixies, the brownies, and the gnomes will be able to make the goblins give back to us all the things they have stolen!"

So that night the rabbit took Ringding the fairy, Twinks the pixie, Frisk the brownie, and Snip the gnome into the kitchen of the dolls' house and shut the door.

"Whatever is the matter?" asked Ringding in alarm, looking at the rabbit's solemn pink face. "You look as if you have lost a new penny and found a broken button!"

"I've something to tell you," said the rabbit, "and I don't want the goblins to hear me. Little folk, I am sorry to say that the goblins have been stealing some of our things."

The little folk stared at the pink rabbit in horror. Could it really be true? Ringding went very red indeed. She felt quite cross.

"I don't believe it," she said. "You have made a mistake, Rabbit."

But when the rabbit told her about his brooch and the red-haired doll's necklace and the walking duck's key, the little folk nodded their heads.

"Yes," said Twinks the pixie. "I believe you, Rabbit. It was only yesterday that I noticed the goblins had a new front door key fitting their lock in the oak tree – and now I come to think of it, it was exactly like the key belonging to the walking duck!"

"What shall we do about it?" said Frisk the brownie.

"We shall have to use some magic on the goblins," said Snip the gnome. "We must make them give up the stolen things somehow."

"But the goblins know more magic than we do," said Ringding. "Whatever spell we do to make them give back what they have stolen will be of no use

– for the goblins know much stronger spells than we do!"

"Well, we will try, anyway," said Snip.

So that night, when the goblins had all gone from the playroom into the garden, the little folk went to the oak tree where the goblin family lived and made a spell to force them to give up the stolen goods. But it was no use at all! The goblins put their heads out of their little window and laughed at them.

"You don't know enough magic!" they shouted. "Stop your silly spells, or we will make a stronger one and turn you into ladybirds!"

The little folk went away. They didn't want to be turned into ladybirds! They told the toys what had happened, and everyone was very sad.

The next night the goblins visited the playroom bold as ever – and do you know, although the toys kept a close watch on them to make sure they did not take anything, those clever goblins managed to steal quite a lot of things.

"Look!" cried the walking duck, peeping into Mummy's work-basket, which she had left in the corner on the floor. "Mummy's little scissors are gone – the ones she cuts buttonholes with!"

"And all her needles!" cried the rabbit, seeing the needle-case quite empty.

"And her nice steel thimble," cried the clockwork mouse. "Oh, whatever will she say?"

"It is time *we* did some magic!" said the rabbit suddenly. "I believe I know how to get back the stolen things. Yes, I believe I do!"

He ran to the toy cupboard and pulled out a big magnet that the children sometimes played with. He and the toys slipped out of the window and ran to the oak tree. They banged on the door, and when the goblins opened it the toys crowded inside.

"Goblins," said the rabbit sternly, "we

have come to get back the things you stole tonight! We have some wonderful magic, much stronger than any *you* know! Watch!"

The rabbit took the big magnet, which he had been holding behind him, and showed it to the goblins. They laughed scornfully.

"That will not find you anything!" they said.

The rabbit held out the magnet, and then a very queer thing happened! The stolen pair of scissors, which had been hidden under the carpet, suddenly flew up to the magnet and hung themselves on the end of it! Then dozens of needles appeared and flew to the magnet, too! They hung there tightly. And then from a goblin's pocket the thimble flew out and rushed to the magnet as well.

"Aha!" said the rabbit, pleased. "You see what powerful magic we keep in the playroom, Goblins!"

The goblins turned pale, as they

stared in surprise. They had never seen a magnet before, and they were full of fear. They rushed to the door, crowded out, and disappeared into the night.

"We shan't see *them* again," said the rabbit pleased. "Let's just look round and see if we can find anything else they stole."

They hunted around and found all the things they had missed, and a few more, too! The walking duck took her key from the front door of the oak tree and tied it on to a new ribbon round her neck. She was very pleased to have it back again.

Then back they all went to the playroom and put the needles, thimble, and scissors into the work-basket. They laughed whenever they thought of the goblins' astonishment.

"That magnet was a fine idea," said the pink rabbit, putting it away in the cupboard. "I don't think the goblins will rob toys again. They will be too much afraid of magic in the playroom."

The dirty old teddy

Once there was an old, old teddy bear in the toy cupboard. He was so old and dirty that nobody knew what colour he had once been, and he didn't even remember himself.

He only had one arm, and one of his legs was loose. His eyes were odd, because one was a black button and the other was brown. He had a hole in his back and sawdust sometimes came out of it. So you can guess he was rather a poor old thing.

But he was wise and kind and loved to make a joke, so the other toys loved him and didn't mind him being so dirty and old.

"All the same, I'm afraid he'll be

thrown away into the dustbin one day," said the blue rabbit, shaking his head. "I'm afraid he will. He really is *so* old and dirty."

The little girl in whose playroom the bear lived never played with the old teddy. She had a fine new one, coloured blue, with a pink ribbon round his neck, two beautiful eyes, and a growl in his middle. She loved him very much. She always pushed the old teddy away if he was near her.

One day her mother picked up the old teddy and looked at him. A little

sawdust dribbled out of the hole in his back.

"Good gracious!" said Joan's mother. "This old teddy really must be thrown away. He isn't even nice enough to be given to the jumble sale."

"Well, throw him away, then," said Joan. "I don't want him. He looks horrid with only one arm and a leg that wobbles, Mummy. I never play with him now."

All the toys listened in horror. What! Throw away the poor old teddy! Oh, dear, what a terrible pity!

"Well, I'll put him in the waste-paper basket in a minute," said her mother. She put the teddy on the table beside her and went on with her knitting. Soon the bell rang for dinner, and Joan's mother forgot about the teddy.

As soon as she had gone out of the room the toys called to the bear, "Hurry, Teddy! Get down from the table and hide at the back of the toy cupboard!"

The bear fell off the table and limped

over to the toy cupboard. He really was very frightened. He hoped that Joan's mother wouldn't remember she had left him on the table.

She didn't remember – because when she came back she had another child with her, besides Joan. A little boy clung to her hand, and she was talking to him.

"You will love staying with us, Peter dear. You shall play with Joan's toys, and have a ride on the rocking-horse."

Peter was Joan's cousin and he had come to stay with Joan for three weeks. He was a dear little boy, but very shy. The toys watched him all the afternoon. He was frightened of the rocking-horse because it was so big. He liked the dolls' house because everything in it was little. He loved the top that spun round and played a tune, and he liked the train that ran on its lines.

When bedtime came, and he sat eating bread-and-milk in the playroom, he began to cry.

"I've left my old monkey behind," he wept. "I always go to bed with him. I shall be lonely without him."

"Well, you shall have one of Joan's toys to take to bed with you," said her mother, and she took him to the toy cupboard. "Choose which you would like, Peter."

Peter picked up the brown dog – and then the rabbit – and then the sailor doll – and then the blue cat. And then, quite suddenly, he saw the dirty old teddy bear looking up at him out of his odd brown and black eyes. He gave a squeal and picked him up.

"Oh, can I have this darling soft teddy? He looks at me so kindly – and I do like his funny eyes. Oh, please, please, may I take *him* to bed with me?"

"Good gracious! It's the bear I meant to throw away in the dustbin!" said Joan's mother. "You don't want a dirty old toy like that, surely!"

"Yes I do – yes I do!" cried Peter, and he hugged the bear hard. "I shall cry if you don't let me have him."

"Of course you shall have him, but if you love him so much I shall have to mend him up a bit tomorrow," said Joan's mother. So Peter took the old teddy to bed with him – and you simply can't imagine how happy the bear was!

He cuddled up to Peter and loved him. It was such a long, long time since he had been taken to bed by anyone. He was so happy that even his little growl came back when Peter pressed his tummy.

And next day – good gracious! Joan's mother took him and made him a new arm. She sewed on his wobbly leg. She mended the hole in his back – and she made him a beautiful blue shirt with little sleeves!

You can't think how different he looked! The other toys looked at him in amazement and joy.

"You won't go into the dustbin now, Teddy," they said. "You look simply lovely!" And he does, doesn't he?

The day the Princess came

"The Princess is coming to visit our village!" shouted Bron the brownie, racing through the streets, waving a letter. "Next week! Hurray! She wants to have tea in one of our cottages! Hurray!"

Well, what an excitement! A meeting was held at once, and all the villagers went to it, of course.

"Now, we must vote for the prettiest, best-kept cottage in our village," said Bron, importantly. "All our cottages are pretty, but not all of them are tidy and clean and well-kept inside. The Princess must have tea in the one that is best inside as well as outside."

So all the villagers voted on bits

of paper and put down the name of the cottage they thought to be the best for the Princess to have tea in.

"I'll count the votes," said Bron, and he did. He looked up, puzzled. "*Two* cottages have exactly the same number of votes!" he said. "Cherry Cottage, where Dame Twinkle lives – and Apple Cottage, where old Mother Quickfeet lives. Exactly the same number of votes each!"

"Well – let the Princess choose which cottage she will have tea in when she comes!" called out Pippitty the pixie. "*We* can't choose. Both cottages are beautiful, inside and out."

So it was left like that – and dear me, how Mother Quickfeet and Dame Twinkle set to work to make their cottages shine and sparkle!

Their gardens were lovely, full of hollyhocks and cornflowers and marigolds and sweet-peas, and there wasn't a weed to be seen. Dame Twinkle got Bron to whitewash her cottage and Mother Quickfeet got Pippitty to paint her shutters a pretty blue.

And dear me, what a lot of work went on inside! Each cottage had just two rooms, a bedroom and a parlour. Up went new curtains, each carpet was beaten till it could have cried, and the floors were polished till they were like mirrors. New cushion-covers were made, flowers were set in every corner, the windows were cleaned over and over again, and the smell of freshly baked pies came out of the open doors of the cottages, and made everyone wish they could go and taste them!

That was the day before the Princess was to visit the village. People came and peeped inside the two cottages, wondering which one the Princess would choose.

"I *think* she'll choose Mother Quickfeet's," said Bron. "She has such a pretty wallpaper, so fresh and flowery."

"Ah, but Dame Twinkle has a

rocking-chair," said Pippitty. "I'm sure the Princess would like to sit in that rocking-chair."

Now that night something happened. The cottage next door to Mother Quickfeet's caught fire. It was a little thatched cottage, and soon the straw roof was sending up big flames to the sky. What a to-do!

"Old Man Surly's cottage is burning!" cried Dame Twinkle, when she went out to take in her washing. Just then Mrs Surly rushed into her own garden and called out loudly.

"We can't save the cottage. My children are frightened. So are the cat and the dog. Please, please will you and Mother Quickfeet take us in for the night?"

Then Mother Quickfeet ran out into *her* garden. Dear, dear, what a to-do! Nothing would save that old cottage now. Well, it was tumbling down anyway, and it was all Mr Surly's fault for never doing anything to put it right!

"You can all go to your uncle's," said Mother Quickfeet. "He's got a nice big house, and he'll take you in."

"But it's night-time, and he lives such a long way away," wept Mrs Surly. "And my baby is ill. Oh, please do let us rest in your two cottages tonight, Mother Quickfeet and Dame Twinkle."

Now there were three boys and girls in the Surly family besides the baby – and, alas, they were not very well brought-up children. They were rough and rather rude. As for the dog, he was a dreadful chewer, and everyone shooed him away if they saw him because he would chew up carpets or shoes or books – anything he came across!

"We can't have you," said Mother Quickfeet, firmly. "It's quite impossible. Surely you know that Mother Twinkle and I are hoping to have the Princess to tea tomorrow, and have got our cottages simply beautiful? No – you go to your uncle's. It's your own fault that the cottage has caught fire. You don't sweep the chimney often enough."

Mrs Surly began to cry. The baby howled. The dog barked. Mr Surly growled, and picked up the baby's cradle, which he had managed to save.

"All right," he said. "We'll go. Maybe we can find someone kinder than you, with your talk of beautiful cottages and lovely princesses!"

The little company set off gloomily down the lane. They passed Mother Quickfeet's cottage, and she kept the door shut fast! They passed Dame Twinkle's, too – but before they had gone very far she was out of her door and at the gate calling loudly.

"Mrs Surly! You can come in here. I can't bear to let you walk all that way to your uncle's in the dark of night. Come along in, all of you!"

Mother Quickfeet opened her door. "*Well!*" she said, "fancy having that rough, bad-mannered family to stay with you the night before the Princess arrives! You must be mad!"

"Well – perhaps I am," said Dame Twinkle. "I can't help it. I just feel so sorry for them all. And anyway they'll be gone tomorrow morning and I can easily clear up after them and make things nice again. Are you sure you won't have one or two of the children tonight, Mother Quickfeet? They'll make such a crowd in my cottage."

"Certainly *not*," said Mother Quickfeet and she slammed her door quickly.

Soon all the Surly family was in Cherry Cottage – and dear me, they certainly filled every corner! What with the baby, three other children, Mr and Mrs Surly, *and* the cat and dog, there didn't seem anywhere to sit or even to stand!

Dame Twinkle made them as comfortable as she could. They were all hungry, so she gave them all the pies and cakes and jam sandwiches she had made for the next day.

"I can easily make some more," she thought. "Oh dear – that dog is chewing my new rug. Shoo, dog, shoo!"

The dog shooed away, and began to chew a cushion. The cat leapt up on the mantelpiece and knocked down the clock – smash!

The three children squashed into the lovely rocking-chair and rocked hard. Creak, creak, crash! One of the rockers broke and down went all the children.

"Oh dear – my lovely rocking-chair," said Dame Twinkle, sadly. "Oh, Mrs Surly, *don't* let the baby pull my flowers out of that vase!"

But the baby did, and after that he crawled to the coal-scuttle, and threw bits of coal all over the place! The dog chewed the bits, and then when anyone walked across the room, crunch-crunch went the bits of chewed-up coal under their feet!

Mr Surly lighted his pipe. Goodness gracious, what a smoke he made, and how horrid it smelt! Mother Twinkle almost cried. Would the smell of smoke have gone from the room before the Princess came?

Next morning Mother Quickfeet looked into Dame Twinkle's cottage. My goodness, what a mess! A dirty floor, torn cushions, a chewed-up carpet, a broken rocking-chair, and everything in a mess and a muddle!

Mother Quickfeet didn't say a word. She went back to her own trim and tidy cottage, smiling. Aha! Dame Twinkle wouldn't *dream* of inviting the Princess in now. That was quite certain. She would come to tea with Mother Quickfeet, in Apple Cottage.

After breakfast Mr Surly fetched a big hand barrow from the greengrocer's. He piled on to it the few things saved from the fire. The baby was set on it, too, and the little family set off down the lane to go to their uncle's.

"Goodbye, dear, kind Dame Twinkle," said Mrs Surly, hugging her. "I do wish I could stay and help you to clean up, but if we don't start off now we'll never get there. I shall *never* forget your kindness."

Poor Dame Twinkle. She looked round her little cottage, and almost cried. So dirty. So untidy. So many things broken – even her beloved rocking-chair. Could she ever get things straight in time?

She tried her best. She scrubbed the floor, and when it was dry she polished it. She washed the cushions and mended them. She put the broken clock away. She called in Pippitty to mend the rocking-chair, but he said it would take a whole week.

"What a mess your place is in," he said. "It was very kind of you to take in that poor family – but, oh dear, how sad just before the Princess was arriving! I'm *sure* she would have chosen you to have tea with, Dame Twinkle."

Dame Twinkle looked round the room sadly. "I shan't bother about it any more," she said. "No matter how hard I work I won't have time to get it nice again now. Mother Quickfeet must have the Princess to tea – her cottage really does look lovely."

So Dame Twinkle didn't try to do much more to her cottage. She was tired out with her disturbed night so, after dinner, she changed her dress, and put on her best one, so that she could stand at her front gate and wave to the Princess, when she came.

Cloppetty-cloppetty-clop! That was the sound of horses' hooves. The Princess was coming, hurrah, hurrah, hurrah! All the villagers lined the road and shouted and cheered, for they loved the beautiful, kind-hearted princess.

Along came the carriage, what a beauty! And there was the princess, lovelier than ever, a shining crown on her golden hair. She bowed this way and that, and looked just as pleased as the cheering people.

"Your Royal Highness, Mother

Quickfeet, whose cottage is the prettiest and best of all, begs you to take a cup of tea with her," said Bron the brownie, bowing low. He guided the carriage horses to Apple Cottage. At the gate stood Mother Quickfeet, looking very grand indeed in plum-coloured silk, smiling all over her face.

"Wait," said the Princess. "It is *Cherry* Cottage I want, not Apple Cottage."

"No, no," said Bron, hurriedly. "You're making a mistake, Your Highness. It's *Apple* Cottage!"

"Listen to me," said the Princess, in a little, high voice that everyone could hear. "On my way here I met a little family. The man was pushing a hand barrow, and a baby was crying in the middle of it. I stopped and asked them what they were doing and where they were going. And do you know what they said?"

"What?" asked everyone, crowding close.

"They said they had lost their house in a fire last night and had asked Mother Quickfeet at Apple Cottage to take them in – and she wouldn't. But they said that Dame Twinkle, at Cherry Cottage, called after them and took them all in, every one!"

"Good old Dame Twinkle!" shouted Pippitty.

"Mrs Surly told me they had made a mess of her beautiful cottage, and she said she was very sorry because she knew Dame Twinkle wanted me to go to have tea with her," went on the Princess. "Where *is* this kind Dame Twinkle?"

"Here she is, here she is!" yelled Bron the brownie, in excitement, and showed the Princess where the kind old woman was standing wonderingly at her front gate.

"Oh, please!" Dame Twinkle said, half-scared. "Oh, please, dear Bron, don't ask the Princess in to tea at my house. It's in *such* a mess!"

"Dear Dame Twinkle, I'm not coming to tea with you today!" called the little Princess. "I know how horrid it is to have visitors when your house is untidy. So I'm going to take you home to tea with *me*, back to the palace. Will you come?"

What an honour for Dame Twinkle! No one in the whole village had *ever* gone to tea with a Princess before.

And there was Dame Twinkle stepping into the royal carriage, blushing red, hardly able to speak a word!

"Next week I'll come and have tea with *you*, Dame Twinkle," said the Princess, loud enough for Mother Quickfeet to hear. "Not because you have a pretty cottage, which is a common enough thing – but because you've a warm, kind heart, and that's quite rare! Now – are you quite comfortable? And do you like meringues for tea, because I know we've got some at the palace?"

Nobody heard what Dame Twinkle answered, because the carriage drove off at that moment, clippitty-clop-clop. Everyone cheered again. They didn't mind the Princess paying such a short visit, because she would be back again the next week. Hurrah!

"Good old Dame Twinkle – she deserves a treat," cried Bron. "Three cheers, everyone!"

And every single person joined in – except Mother Quickfeet, who had gone quietly back into her beautiful cottage to cry.

Oh dear – what could she do now? Well – she could go and tidy up Dame Twinkle's cottage, and bake her some pies to welcome her when she came back.

Do you suppose she did? I do hope so.